The Many Faces of Love . . .

"Desmond," Dragon said, "would you please take off that ugly shirt?"

She undid the buttons and slipped her arms out of the sleeves as Dragon took it from her.

"Beautiful!" he whispered. "Beautiful!" He put his hands around her slender waist and held her. "Desmond, have you ever made love?"

She shook her head.

"You've never been with a man?"

She bit her lip, then buried her head against his chest. "There was a boy, back on Barbados," she said into his shirt. "Oh, Dragon, I'm so ashamed!"

"Desmond, look at me."

She lifted her tear-strewn face.

"I will show you what love is, my darling." He picked her up and carried her to a level stretch of beach, where he gently laid her down. . . .

Later she said, "Dragon, promise me you won't tell them I'm a girl, or they'll all be after me!"

"Of course I promise. So right now, start acting again—like a boy."

His words were a stern command. Only his soft eyes betrayed him.

The Privateer's Woman

June Wetherell

PINNACLE BOOKS   LOS ANGELES

THE PRIVATEER'S WOMAN

An original Pinnacle Books edition, published for the first time anywhere.

ISBN: 0-523-40186-8

First printing, February 1978

Cover illustration by Bruce Minnet

Printed in the United States of America

PINNACLE BOOKS, INC.
One Century Plaza
2029 Century Park East
Los Angeles, California 90067

The Privateer's Woman

1.

"Boy—get down here!"

Desmond, blond hair blowing in the wind, looked down from high in the rigging. The men on deck had shrunk to pigmies, their bandannas, their broad brimmed hats, even their cutlasses were almost toy-size. This was the place to be, seated on the cross trees, in your own world of sky and wind. The ship was at anchor in calm waters; there was a sense of well-being in the gentle sway at the top. It was almost like being a bird, free and independent, breathing the clean salt-scented air instead of deck and cabin odors of rum, tobacco, sweat, and often blood.

From here the buccaneers formed a pattern of flamboyant color, nice little fellows dressed up like dandies, the sun glinting on their cutlasses and their pistols and their earrings. One was not close enough to smell them, to see their matted grimy hair, their scars, the missing hand or ear, the greasy blood-stained pantaloons.

The youngest, the smallest, the most agile, Desmond frequently was sent up the rigging to keep watch for other ships, or to hoist the skull and crossbones, But, when no ships were sighted, when no flag need be flown, the cabin boy was kept busy swabbing the decks, cleaning the pistols, or sharpening the cutlasses, gutting fish or birds in the galley, filling the rum bottles from the big cask in the cellar, cleaning muck from anywhere it appeared.

Desmond did the work, shared a small bit in the loot when a ship was captured, ate what the rest of them ate and for the most part was not mistreated. Sent on fools' errands sometimes, just so the rest of the crew could sit there guzzling rum and laughing their heads off. But the voice of the quartermaster, calling out just now, had had a different tone. Sharp, angry, threatening.

One hand was lifted to indicate the command had been heard, then Desmond turned and started the slow descent. A long-ago fall from the rigging, only a few feet above the deck, had caused enough pain to ingrain a habit of care. More care going down than in climbing up.

"Damn you, hurry!" the officer was calling again.

What mistake could I have made? Desmond wondered. What did I forget to do? Am I in for a beating?

It was late afternoon and the ship was at anchor. Most of the crew were on deck, leaning against the sides or squatting as they swizzled rum. They looked up as Desmond descended, an amused audience, as if they knew why Desmond had been called down so peremptorily.

"Yes, sir?" Desmond waited, trying not to show fright. *I should not be afraid. To the best of my knowledge I've done nothing wrong.*

Batham, the quartermaster, had only one eye, but it made up in malignity for the missing one now covered with a patch.

He did not speak immediately. He stood there in ominous silence, looking over Desmond as if that poor infortunate were a slave he was considering purchasing. His contempt hung in the air between them.

"My boy . . ." The words had no touch of kindness usually held by such a phrase. "My boy, it is time you learned to fight."

Desmond had longed for this moment. It meant acceptance by the crew, it meant not being shoved aside when they captured a ship, but being allowed to join. And, most important, to receive a man's instead of a boy's share of the booty.

"I can wield a cutlass, sir." Eagerly. "I learned on the plantation. I cut sugar cane and small trees and they told me I was very good. May I show you?"

"I wasn't speaking of a cutlass. Any fool can slash about with a cutlass. Besides, you are too slight for that. First, the sword."

He pulled one from its scabbard, a weapon

scarcely long enough to be called a sword. It was more like a stubby long dagger.

"As a young gentleman on that plantation, were you taught fencing?"

"I was not a young gentleman!" Desmond blurted. "My mother was . . . a servant. No, I was not taught to fence."

The sword. Sharp, sinister. Here, in front of those mocking pirates, would not be the place to learn. And not from that quartermaster who obviously, for reasons of his own, despised his cabin boy.

The officer tossed the sword, flipping the handle over, and miraculously Desmond caught it. Then the officer reached for his own weapon. Longer, sharper.

"On guard!" He was in position.

Desmond had played at sword fights with the "young gentlemen" on that plantation who *were* taught fencing, had watched some of the lessons, and had some idea of what was supposed to go on. Not easy, when you were trembling; only possible with the now engulfing bravado of fear. There were no buttons on the sword tips here.

"On guard!" A high-pitched echo of the officer's tone.

Desmond was agile. A tree climber, now a rope climber, arms and legs were under perfect control. Batham was bigger but clumsier. And Desmond began to realize that first, the man had been drinking rum, and second, that he was not fighting to kill. He was fighting as if he were playing a game. It was his method of wordless teaching. One should be grateful, one should regard it as a game and forget the expression on the quartermaster's face when he first said, *you must learn to fight*.

I will really be one of them now, Desmond thought. When they clamber over a prize vessel I shall be with them, sword in hand.

Whenever there was a successful parry of one of Batham's thrusts there was a roar from the pirates. Was it laughter, or was it an ironic cheer?

They circled around and around the deck in a rhythm that was almost like a dance, Desmond's slender bare feet whisking, over and over again, just out of the other's reach.

Then suddenly the dance Desmond was beginning to enjoy was shattered. A sudden lunge and Batham's heavier sword caught and swirled the lighter blade out of Desmond's hand and came straight for the heart.

Desmond leaped back but not quickly enough. The sword did not touch the flesh but it ripped open the shirt.

Her breasts—her small young breasts she had tried so hard to hide—were there in the heavy gold of the afternoon light, for all to see.

For two years Desmond Duval had been pretending to be a boy. Her yellow hair, bleached by the sun, had been hacked off shoulder length, as short as a man's. Her body, trim and slim, fit well into trousers and shirt, except for those breasts which lately had started to grow.

She would never forget the night she ran away from the plantation on Barbados, the long, long walk to the waterfront, sitting on the dock, hidden behind a barrel, waiting for the dawn.

She spent several nights on that tar and salt-scented dock. Each day she mingled with the seamen—old and young, some with rings in their noses, some with pigtails, some with long curly whiskers, all walking clumsily, as if their feet were unused to land.

Some of the ships were navy, others full-crewed merchant ships. She tried them all, but nobody wanted a cabin boy.

Until one very dark night when a strange ship without a flag slipped into the harbor and anchored far out. A few men came ashore in a small boat. She watched them raiding a warehouse, and then they spotted her and asked her to help them. "Come on, lad, take a load there—we'll see you're repaid." And so she had helped them, load after load, and then, suddenly, while she was still aboard ship, a torch was spotted on the dock and the ship unfurled its sails and moved away.

The *Lady May*. A pirate ship!

Some of the food they had taken from the warehouse was spread out for a feast—salt pork, biscuits, brandy, pickled fruit—and ravenous, she had eaten with them and they had accepted her and adopted her as a member of the crew.

Until this moment when the shirt was ripped from her body Desmond had been sure she had fooled them. Now she realized that the quartermaster must have guessed her secret and chosen this way of revealing it to his mates. Clutching her shirt in front of her, she stood there defiant, looking at one face and then another. It was a man's world and when she was thought to be a male, everything had been all right. Now all had changed. The pirates' eyes had become the eyes of predatory beasts.

"I've done my job well, haven't I?" she asked.

Batham laughed. "You've done a boy's job, yes. But you haven't done *your* job. Not yet."

She knew all too well what he meant, what they all meant. She could not fight the lot of them, she could not hope that one of them would defend her.

Yet, even as her good sense told her she was helpless, she inadvertently took a step away from the officer.

His long arm shot out and grabbed hers, the one holding the shirt in front of her. He did not speak, he just held her firm.

"Try to get away from me. Just try, and you'll have the beating of your life."

A cheer rose from the pirates. "Rum! More

rum!" one of them cried and others echoed. "Rum! Rum!" and there was the noise of empty bottles splashing overboard.

The quartermaster, gripping her arm so tightly that it hurt, told her, "Fetch rum. Fast!"

He let go of her, as he pushed her in the direction of the hold.

As she hurried past, two or three of the men reached out to grab at her breasts or pinch her buttocks.

"Wait!" A command from the officer. "Time enough for that!"

She got past them and started down the ladder into the darkness of the hold. She ran toward the huge keg of rum and then stopped. She reversed the shirt, back to front, and tied the ragged part behind her.

Then she began filling the bottles that lined the walls. *They want rum. I'll give them rum! I'll get them sodden, the way the master was each night back on Barbados. They'll never get me, none of them!*

Yet all the while her mind was racing with the possibilities of what might happen. Two of them would hold her while a third one . . . no, the quartermaster wouldn't let them, he wanted her for himself. But only first, she remembered. Some of the rum spilled from the spigot as she filled a bottle too full.

From the deck she could hear them calling, "Rum! Rum! rum!" like birds cawing in the morning light.

She carried an armload of bottles up the ladder and set them on the deck. Batham was right there at the top of the ladder, waiting for her.

He grabbed her arm, but as she tugged to get away there was noise from the other side of the deck, the sound of scuffling.

Batham yelled out, "Stop that! Here's your rum!"

A few of the men moved forward but the two who had started to fight did not.

Batham dropped her arm and ran to intervene.

Desmond turned and as fast as she could, ran to the quarterdeck and along in the dark to the very end. She swung herself up on the rail.

The sun had set and the swift tropical dark covered the star-specked sky. Land looked a long way away, only a row of dark blobs of hills against the faintly lit sky.

There was nothing to do but swim for it. She prayed silently that somewhere over there was a beach, that it was not all rocks against the sea.

There was one feeble light along the shoreline, no bigger than a landlocked star, but it was *something* on . . . why, she did not even know the name of the island! All she knew was that she was somewhere north of Barbados in the West Indies.

She climbed the rail and jumped over the side, terribly aware of the sound when she struck the water, hoping it would not be audible to the men on deck.

Sharks? The boys back on Barbados had talked about sharks, way out where it was deep, especially in the dark . . .

There was a strange light in the water that draped her arms with silver. Would they be able to see her, from the ship? So far she had heard no uproar, no one was calling after her. Perhaps it would take a while, with all that rum, before they started to look for her.

A flare in the sky behind her. Someone had lighted a torch. She slipped under water, down and down, held her breath for as long as possible. The shirt, torn earlier, washed free and floated away.

At last she surfaced. The flare was gone. Again she started swimming in the direction of that small light, long, slow, steady strokes; she must not get frantic and try too hard or she would soon be exhausted. Now and then she would stop for a bit, treading water, turning to look back at the ship. It was the only way she could tell how far she had gone—the land seemed as distant as ever, but the ship, thank God, was growing smaller.

The stars faded and the water, the sky, the whole world was consumed by black. The rain came first in such small drops that they might have been part of the foam. Then the drops grew in size and intensity, pelting down on the ocean with a roar of power; she could only try to go on steadily swimming. But the wind was whipping the water into crests that swept her with them—she could only pray it was in the direction of the shore.

She was getting tired; never had she swum so far, never in such an ocean. But still she kept on, doggedly, stubbornly, blindly. No longer was there any light visible anywhere.

Without warning a bigger wave, a mountain of water, swept over her and tossed her as if she were a piece of driftwood. She felt herself rise to the top of the wave and then tumble down and down until she was slammed against a boulder, and knew she had reached the shore.

At first she lay flat on her face trying to cling to the land. Land? It was nothing but shifting rocks, and each time the waves came they tried to pull her back into the sea, but each time the waters receded she managed to crawl another few feet forward.

The rain stopped, the stars began reappearing, and at last she reached a patch of sand, above the surf, above the water line. She burst into tears of gratitude and then, exhausted, she lost consciousness.

She could feel the sun on her back. It was morning. Then someone took her by the shoulders.

"Wake up, boy, wake up!"

She was turned over. She looked up into a

man's face. He was staring at her bare breasts in bewilderment as he took his hands from her shoulders.

He was a stocky old white man, almost bald, with big ears silhouetted in the sunlight.

She managed, "Who are you? Where am I?"

"Who are you, that's the question."

"Where am I?" she asked again, like a lost child.

"At the distillery. On Cabra. I'm Obediah Jackson."

She tried to sit up but fell back again. She brushed her hand across her face. She was scratched, from head to toe, and the scratches were stinging.

He asked, "What happened?"

What happened? Where to begin? Finally she said, "I . . . jumped overboard."

"I see." His smile was kindly. "Don't try to talk, lass, not yet. We'll get you up to the house. I'm sure old Peg will find something for your cuts."

He straightened up, cupped his hands around his mouth and bellowed, "Buck!"

A moment later a large black fellow was running toward them, wide-eyed. Desmond rolled over, more awake now, and becoming embarrassed.

"There's been a little accident. "Obediah's voice was dry. "Take her up to the house."

Obediently the black man nodded, swooped

down, picked her up easily in his long arms and moved up the beach.

The house was no more than a shack, standing back from what she now saw was a very small beach. The thatched-roof building was on stilts. Next to it was a more substantial stone building with a huge chimney from which black smoke was pouring. The distillery, he had said. Rum. It made her remember last night.

Buck laid her on a straw mat on the shack's patch of porch, and soon the woman called Peg was bending over her. Peg, black as the man called Buck, seemed to be the mistress of the place. Trotting at her heels was a small coffee-colored lad with ears exactly like Obediah's.

Peg's hands were gentle as she removed the ragged wet pants and handed them to Buck who hung them on a clothesline strung over the porch, while Peg washed all the scratches, patted on an ointment that first stung and then soothed, then threw a ragged but spotless sheet across Desmond.

Obediah, who had disappeared during Peg's nursing, reappeared with a coconut shell in one hand which he held toward Desmond. She could smell the rum. She shook her head.

"Drink it. You need it. Fresh. New. Still warm from the still. Will cure . . . anything."

She took a sip. It burned her lips and her tongue, and went down her throat like a red-hot knife. But after a moment, after choking

13

and sneezing, she did feel more alive. Enough to sit up, wrapping the sheet around her.

"Thank you," she told Obediah.

"Feel better?"

"Oh, yes!"

He sat down across from her and slowly lit his pipe.

"Better enough to tell me now, what happened?"

"I . . . I guess so."

"You really ought to. Before I . . . and Peg, and Buck, and even Charlie, the little nipper here, all die of curiosity. It isn't every day that a . . . young lady is washed up on our beach."

"Young lady," she repeated. "I've never been called that before!"

"What do you call yourself?"

"For two years I've called myself a boy."

"Oh. That accounts . . ." he pointed, ". . . for the pantaloons."

She nodded. "I've been a cabin boy, you see."

"But you jumped ship. I think I can guess why. Someone discovered you really were a cabin girl."

"That's it."

"Did anyone . . ." He puffed on his pipe, looking embarrassed. "Did anyone . . . harm you?"

She shook her head. "No. They were drinking rum. I got away." She gave a little shudder. "I

14

was scared, sir. I really was. But I got away!" she finished proudly.

"And now you're going home."

"Home?"

"I'm guessing again. You ran away from home."

Desmond lifted her head. Her bright black eyes were full of fire. "I won't go back! My mother was a—servant! I was no better than a slave!"

2.

Desmond had grown up playing with the master's sons on the Forrester plantation where her mother was a white slave, on Barbados. No one had even tried to train her how to be a lady. She was just one of the children. The boys had treated her like one of them; teaching her to swim, to fish, to hunt, to play all their games. They only had begun to spurn her when she began to exceed them in every way—even at reading, for she would sneak into the back of the room when their tutor came for his weekly visit.

It was when they started to reject her, that she began to be aware of the differences. The boys had horses, but she was not allowed to ride, except on one of the donkeys. The boys had a big house and rich parents and titles. What did she have? Nothing.

Her mother's job was that of overseer for the black female slaves on the Forrester plantation. When Desmond started to grow up, there seemed to be no real place for her in the household. The Forresters decided that Desmond was not to be trained to be a maid, yet she was not cast down with the blacks. She helped her mother with sewing and mending, and taking care of the linen closet, a corner of which was Desmond's "room."

She had no place in the world. She had nobody but her mother. And when she asked her mother, "What will become of me?" her mother sighed and shook her head.

Desmond's mother, whose name was Maria, was half-Indian, half-Spanish. *Her* mother had sold Maria into slavery to get rid of her.

In spite of such treachery, Maria seemed to have fond memories of the woman. She had told Desmond about her grandmother. "She was small and round and would have been beautiful if her forehead had not been flattened at birth, the way all the Indians' heads are—flattened with a board tied on the forehead." Her ankles had been bound, too, as young girls' ankles were—to make plump legs. "Thank God my head was not flattened," Maria had concluded, "nor my ankles bound. Because my father was not a Carib."

"Who was your father?" Desmond has asked.

"A Spanish soldier. That's all I know. A cruel Spanish soldier who took my mother against her will."

Maria was also small and round but her head was big and her features Spanish, like her father's.

Maria told Desmond, "You have your grandmother's sharp black eyes. And her beautiful

17

teeth. You inherited the best of her. The rest of you . . . is your father."

Maria often talked about Desmond's father, always her eyes were glowing. A French sailor, handsome, so handsome, so good, so gentle. She had known him only a short time.

"When he sailed away he did not know about you, my child. Wherever he is today, if he is still alive, he does not know about you."

Desmond began thinking more and more about herself and what would become of her. She resented her mother's resignation, almost as much as she resented the rich Forresters.

She was sitting on the back porch one twilight when Alan Forrester rode up, swung off his horse, let the stable boy take it, and came striding toward the house, cracking his whip at fireflies.

"Alan?" He was the oldest of the boys, the same age as she. She had always liked Alan best.

"Huh?" He hesitated, frowning down at her. He was a husky boy with big hands and big feet, and a pouting, almost feminine lower lip.

"I haven't seen you lately. What have you been doing?"

"Hunting with my father and my Uncle George." His voice was proud, he had been out with adults.

"Was it fun?"

He shrugged and turned away.

18

One way by which she could always get Alan's attention was with a challenge.

There was a big turpentine tree, arched red-brown, like a statue, on the edge of the woods behind the house.

Desmond got to her feet.

"I'll bet I can beat you up to the naked Indian!"

He turned back.

"Bet you can't!" he snapped.

Desmond already had started running.

She could hear him behind her but she had a good head-start, and reached the tree ahead of him.

She leaned against the tree to face him, raising her clasped hands above her head in triumph.

When he reached her he stood looking at her, his eyes narrowing, a most peculiar expression on his face.

"I won! I won the bet!" she cried. "I beat you!"

Slowly she lowered her arms, because of his expression.

He pushed her away from the tree, toward the woods.

"Alan, what are you doing?"

He grabbed her by both arms. So he wanted to wrestle!

They had wrestled many a time and it had been a fairly even match. She supposed he wanted to wrestle because she had beat him in the race. She laughed as she wiggled free, but he grabbed her again.

"Alan, it's too dark in here, let's . . ."

He paid no attention. He lunged for her leg and she stumbled over a rock, and before she could defend herself he had her flat on her back and was holding her shoulders tightly.

"All right, you win! You win!" she told him.

Still he paid no attention. He threw himself down upon her and started to kiss her. She jerked her head from side to side and pummeled his chest but he had the weight on her. She screamed and one fat hand covered her mouth, the other brutally pulled her legs apart under her shift and kept them apart with his knees. Then he fumbled with his trousers, and with great force thrust himself inside her. The pain was greater than anything she had known in all her life.

Perhaps it only lasted a few minutes but it seemed a lifetime and when she was free at last she heard him laugh.

As he moved away from her she looked up and saw his two younger brothers standing beside him.

"My turn!" one of them cried. "My turn, Alan!"

She dragged herself to a sitting position and screamed again, louder this time. The sound tore through the twilight. She reached beside her and found a rock and threw it, and then another.

One of them cried out and then they all turned and ran out of the woods.

It took quite awhile for her to pull herself together and stagger down the hill and inside the house. She went directly to the linen closet where her mother was at work stacking sheets on the shelves.

Desmond threw herself down on her bed and began to cry. In a moment her mother was beside her, her hand on Desmond's shoulder.

"What is it, child?"

She could only stammer out a few words. "Alan . . . the woods . . ." But she was sure her mother could guess what had happened. She did not scold, nor did she sympathize. She was her calm, practical self, bringing soap and water and ointments and an old Indian medicine to help Desmond sleep.

"It was awful, Mother, it was so awful, what he did to me! Is it always like that?" Desmond wept.

"No, child, no."

"Is that what love is?" Desmond wanted to know. "If it is, I don't want ever, ever to be in love!"

"That was not love," Maria shook her head, "Someday you will know what love is, what it can be. Some day you will find a man, like your father, a gentle man, who will know how and where to touch you, to teach you what love is. Some day, if you are patient, you will find that man. But you must accept your fate, Desmond.

21

You must know that no one will ever marry you. You are fair-skinned, you may yet become a beautiful woman, but there is no place for you except, if you are lucky, to be some rich man's mistress. You are an outcast, as I am. Be thankful you are not black. You will escape many beatings, much cruelty. But you must understand you will never have real freedom. It's a man's world."

"Why? Why?" Desmond wanted to know.

"You were born a woman. It is God's way. And right now you must be careful. Very careful."

Careful! Of course she was, after that. But her bitterness deepened. All she could think of was getting out of that house and running away. But how? Where?

She never went outside alone after dark, until one evening when she knew the whole family had gone into town to a party. She stepped outside and began pacing back and forth, near the house, in the moonlight. She stopped to look down toward the water where the boats were anchored. If only she could sail away in one of them!

Then, by chance, one of the servants spoke to her out of the night. When she answered the man said, "Sorry, Miss Desmond, I thought it was one of the young masters."

That was when the idea came to her. Her mother had said it was a man's world, and therefore it was a boy's world. If she had been born a boy everything would have been different. Men of all kinds came to the West Indies, nobody asked where they came from or why. A nobody could become a somebody by hard work. She knew she was healthy, strong, and clever as any male. She would simply pretend to be a boy. Maybe then she could sign on on a ship.

First she must steal someone's clothes.

Alan's clothes? It would serve him right!

When her mother was in bed, when the other servants had left the house and gone to their quarters, she found her way through the house to the bedrooms. The Forresters were still out, and she passed door after door until she found Alan's room. She had been in there often enough when they were younger, and now she found pants and shirt, took them back to her room, and hid them under her palm leaf mattress.

Next she stole quietly to the kitchen for bread and cheese, and hid those beside the clothes.

She stayed awake in her room until she heard the Forresters return, then when the house was again quiet she tiptoed into her mother's room and found her mother's precious sewing shears, which she took back to her own room.

By moonlight, in front of her small, scratchy mirror, she slashed off her long hair and tucked it under the mattress in place of the clothes and the food.

And left the house forever.

"I'll never be back!" she told Obediah now. "I'll never be a slave!"

Obediah's voice was deadly quiet. "I was a slave, once. They were pleased to call me an indentured servant, but for seven long years I worked for food and shelter, and I was treated . . . no better than they treat the blacks." He looked over at Peg, who was sitting in a corner of the porch, sewing in her lap. Still looking at her, he went on. "I, at least, had a chance to work my way to freedom. They even gave me ten whole pounds at the end. I had a chance, which few blacks ever get. So I . . . endured."

Peg said, "I ran away, sire. As she did. I had no choice."

"It's because we're women!" Desmond sat up straighter. "Women have to run!"

Obediah looked at her for a long moment. His funny old face was thoughtful. He seemed to be taking his time before he spoke. Finally he asked, "What's your name, child?"

"Desmond. Desmond Duval."

"French?"

"My father was."

"Did your father teach you to speak French?"

"I never knew my father!" She said angrily.

"He never even knew he was my father," she added bitterly. "I'm nobody, and I have nowhere to go."

She sank back on the straw mat.

Obediah leaned over and touched her shoulder.

"And you're exhausted. Try to sleep. Try not to think. Not yet."

She sighed. "Thank you!" Then she added, "You're very kind."

He walked away and she fell asleep.

She felt safe there at Obediah's. For the first time since childhood, when safety had been taken for granted. She knew she could not stay on forever, but for the time being she accepted their generosity. She ate and slept and ate and slept again.

It was on the second morning that she asked if it would be all right if she went down alone to the beach, to bathe.

Peg produced a bar of home-made soap and a rough towel. Desmond wrapped the towel around her for a robe. Her pants were dry and mended, and Peg had cut down one of Obediah's heavy cotton shirts, so Desmond rolled them into a bundle and took them alone, for after her bath.

The beach was so different from the morning she had awakened there. The turquoise waters were calm, the waves little bits of froth lapping the sand.

She did her best to make lather in the salt water, then put the bar of soap aside and started swimming.

Now swimming was a pleasure again, as the clear water caressed her. She swam, then lay on her back and rested. She could hear pelicans diving, one after another, splashing into the water, and the cries of their little parasites, the booby birds. And there was the sound of Buck chopping wood for the fire in the kiln.

She was lying on her back when she heard another sound. Oars. She lifted her head. A sloop was in the little bay, a black man rowing a gig ashore. In it sat a white man, staring at her.

3.

It was a small, unpretentious church, but its high arched ceiling, its thick stone walls and windows, uncluttered by glass, suited its tropical setting. Lilias wondered if some of the congregation only came because it was cool inside. The church was set high on the side of Mount Cuerno, the highest part of the island of Cabra. There was always a breeze, swooping up from the waters of Sir Francis Drake channel and flowing through the open windows from one side of the church to the other, ruffling the bonnets of the few ladies.

Up behind the mahogany pulpit, hand-carved by one of the slaves, her husband Ian droned on in Latin. Lilias did not even try to listen. She never had. The words of the service, even the English ones, meant little to her. She much preferred the hymn singing. Particularly here on Cabra, when the few blacks who were allowed to stand at the rear of the chapel joined in. Their voices were rich and harmonious, in contrast to the voices of the handful of whites—planters and merchants and their families—who usually sang in a lackluster off key, whereas the blacks sang as if they meant every unintelligible word. They sang from their souls and it was both beautiful—and sad.

But now, while Ian slipped from Latin into English, without changing his intonation or clarifying the import of his words, his audience sat in polite, constrained silence, their expressions blank, their hands folded, as if they were all doing penance for a week of normal living.

A branch of bougainvillaea swung delicately against the side of the window nearest to her, a blend of pink and orange, sheer as fine cotton or bits of writing paper, dainty and ephemeral, but daringly perseverant. Sunday is like any other day to that plant, Lilias thought. For her Sunday, although afflicted with the church service, had its compensations. For one thing, it granted her the privilege of putting on her best frock, brown silk fluted with lace, with a bodice that fit well, if more modestly than she would have preferred. Part of her trousseau. Her Aunt Rachel had said, over and over, "Remember you are going to be a parson's wife. You must dress properly."

Aunt Rachel never had guessed her niece would some day be living on a British colonial island in the West Indies. Aunt Rachel was a Royalist. A king could do no wrong. If Charles II and James II wanted to Catholicize the Church of England, then that was the way it had to be. After the Bloodless Revolution and the coming of Protestant William and Mary in 1689, Aunt Rachel's loyalty to the crown was strained, but she kept her misgivings to herself.

Before the revolution Ian, like many other clergymen, had left the Church of England and gone his own way. That was the main reason for Aunt Rachel's disapproval of him. Lilias thought it had been a brave thing for him to have done. But she had not guessed that not only had he left the Church but that he would leave England, ship out as a chaplain on a ship, leaving her to wait until he had found a place for himself in the New World.

She kept her eyes on the branch of bougainvillaea. Beautiful. She must remember all the beauty around her, forget what she did not like about this lonely little island which now was home. Forget the mud that came after sudden heavy rain, forget the mosquitoes, the sun that burned her pale skin. But above all forget the loneliness. Forget, too, the planters' wives—only a few lived on Cabra—who treated her with polite, respectful indifference, and the sullen-faced blacks whose language, ostensibly English, she could not understand. And the hours when Ian was off riding about the island in his donkey cart, calling on his parishioners, or sailing his sloop to the out islands to see even more parishioners.

She remembered the letters Ian had written her about Cabra, while she was still in England. He had been right, of course, about the emerald blue waters, about the magnificent green hills thrusting into the Dresden-blue sky, and the clouds that sailed along the horizon in the shapes of gods and goddesses and fairy tale animals. And the endless summertime and the fruits—bananas, mangoes, sugar apples, papayas. And the flowers, wild and tamed—oh, Ian could write beautiful letters. She had imagined herself living in a mansion, waited upon hand and foot.

There were servants. Ian had had to buy two slaves to run the little house—slaves he had immediately freed and to whom he paid salaries. There was a man to work in the flower and vegetable gardens, a woman to haul water, clean the little house, launder in the nearby stream, and cook. But the cooking was definitely not English style. Strange concoctions full of spices, the meat (frequently goat) very tough. And Lilias, who had never been trained to do so much as boil water, was in no position to train the woman—called Zula—to cook in any other way than the one she knew.

And, above all, Lilias could not get used to living out in the country.

She had been born and raised in the heart of London. Her father had been killed in 1672 in the war with the Dutch, the year she was born. Her mother had died in childbirth. Aunt Rachel, the proud widowed aristocrat who had raised Lilias to be a lady, had not thought the young clergyman a suitable match at all.

Lilias never would have met Ian, never fallen in love with him, if she had not had that bout with the fever and Aunt Rachel taken her out to Essex, to recuperate in the country air.

Ian had been the chaplain on the country estate where they were visiting.

She met Ian in the great house, where he lived. She remembered that boyishly smooth face, those great gray eyes, across the dining table. The face seemed more the face of a scholar than a man of piety.

She took her eyes now from the bougainvillaea and looked up at her husband, trying to recall the first moment when she really fell in love with him, when there had been magic and promise in his touch.

And then he answered her unspoken question for her, by announcing communion.

She was not sitting in the front row—where she was supposed to be—because she had come late, spending much too long arranging her hair. Who knew what interesting person might be in attendance that morning, what newcomer off a ship, or visitor from down island, there might be? And, of course, *he* would come to church. *He* always did. She watched the congregation starting in the front row, left to right, one by one each approaching the altar for that scrap of bread (one of Zula's worst efforts) and watered wine from Ian's skimpy wine cellar.

Communion. It had repulsed her ever since its meaning was first explained to her. The blood and the body of Christ. What an ugly thought! she had always gone through the ceremony because it was something one did, but she had always hated it. She remembered that morning in the tiny chapel back in Essex. Only the family going up to the miniature altar where Ian was standing. Aunt Rachel and herself were last, as guests. She was not yet recovered from the fever. She had moved slowly and hesitantly knelt. When it was time to rise she had suddenly found her legs trembling. Then Ian reached down and put his hand under her elbow and helped her to her feet.

The touch. That was all it was, just the touch, but in that moment a feeling shot through her such as she had never known before; it was as if her whole body were on fire.

Strange, because it never had been like that again. She had expected to be caught up by something bigger than herself, bigger than the universe, to be consumed by that fire. She had waited, all during his timorous courtship, for that feeling to return. He vowed his love for her, but his kiss was gentle. And even on their wedding night, the magic did not reappear. He was ever good and sweet and kind and gentle; he called her "my little Lilias," he was forever taking care of her, as if she were a child. He would look at her with those big eyes full of love, but never passion.

Then he went away, hastily, while she was still a bride. Again she had waited and hoped that the separation would make the difference, that when she came to him after months, when they met all over again in a tropical paradise, it would be different.

But it wasn't.

She watched the others moving up the aisle between the benches. Governor Appleby and his stiff-necked, but flouncy wife. Roderick Gresham, the richest planter on the island—big, handsome, male—oh, so very male!—looking strangely subdued in a church. Beside him was his hawk-nosed, imperious, bejeweled wife Rowena—uncrowned queen of Cabra. Then came straight-backed Jonathan Kincaid, only a clerk at Government House, but so much more. An intelligent man. A scholar. Such pleasant company.

But her eyes went back to Roderick Gresham, as they always did. She had scarcely exchanged more than a few words at a time with him, but she vividly remembered each time they met.

She watched them go, one by one, until it was her turn to walk down the aisle.

In a moment like this she felt more secure, closer to being content with life. Her figure was trim and dainty. She walked as Aunt Rachel had taught her—like a queen on her way to being crowned. Her smooth brown hair was arranged tastefully and only partly covered by a scarf. Her chin was up. I am Mrs. Ian Everett, the parson's wife. I am someone of importance.

When she knelt and looked up and met her husband's eyes he smiled, faintly, in exactly the same way he had smiled at all his parishioners. She felt as if he were experiencing as hollow an emotion as she was. This rigmarole can't really mean anything to him, she thought, no more than it does to me. Why does he go on with the charade?

Communion finished, hymnbooks were opened to the proper places and the congregation relaxed into music. Lilias moved her lips as if she were singing but she preferred just to listen. She loved music and there was so little of it here on the island, beyond human voices. There were the birds, of course. *The voice of the turtle was heard in the land.* Each morning at dawn. And sometimes the slaves—only sometimes—sang at their work. But it was always mournful music.

It was when the hymn was finished and there was that moment of silence before Ian began the closing prayer that she heard another sound, from the direction of the open window.

All other heads were bent in prayer but Lilias lifted hers, twisted her neck to look out the window beside her.

It was a wild goat. An old billy goat, perched on one of the big rocks as if he wished to get a better view of the interior of the church. He stared at her, unabashed, his cold close-set eyes disguising his curiosity, as if he were saying, this is my world, what are you doing here?

34

She never had had such a close look at a goat before; always they had scurried away. She somehow did not feel that she was looking at an animal; there was something familiar in his expression. Then, abruptly, she caught the resemblance and almost laughed. Governor Appleby with his big nose and his colorless stupid eyes, even his scraggly beard, might have been standing outside that window.

Would Ian laugh, if she told him about it? Probably not. Ian had an irritating way of never saying anything unkind about anybody.

"Amen." The chorus of many voices, echoed about the small room in toneless relief.

Lilias slipped her hymnbook back in its rack and got to her feet, smoothing her paniers and adjusting the hoops under the paniers. Hoops were too warm for this climate, but Lilias felt sure she was too thin to go without them—even if few other women bothered—for the skirt would not hang right. Besides, Aunt Rachel had always told her, "No lady appears in public without her hoops!"

She had just reached the aisle as the Greshams were coming down. Mrs. Gresham gave her one of those polite, restrained nods of recognition, the token, the duty acknowledgment, all that was required. Roderick Gresham's black eyes swept over Lilias from the top of her head to the hem of her full skirt, lingering there as if hoping to catch a glimpse of her ankles. Then he nodded, and smiled. If she

35

had met him on the street and he had smiled the way he did she might have called it insolent. But she told herself, you are imagining, because you have heard of his reputation with women. It is not insolence, it is more—intimacy. She lowered her eyes.

The Greshams stepped aside to allow her to pass to take her stand by the door.

For a moment she stood alone outside in the glare of the midday sun, watching the sleepy carriage and cart drivers stir themselves awake. Ian had promised her a carriage "some day" but right now they must think of the poor in the parish. He was so generous to the poor! *They* must make do with a donkey and cart.

But I feel beholden to them, Lilias thought. People here look down on me, the other women in particular. I am only the poor parson's wife.

In a moment Ian was beside her. He arrived, breathless as usual, having slipped out the side door and around the church.

The governor and his wife were the first to come by. Their nods gave the impression that it was Ian who was being honored by their presence. The governor's wife always looked peevish. She hated the island and made no bones about it, behaving continually as if they had been committed to prison and as anxious for her husband to finish his sentence so that they could be free to go back to civilization.

The rest continued to file by, saying no more than good day, to gather down in the churchyard in busy talkative little groups. The sermon itself meant nothing to them; going to church was the one real social event of the week. Other affairs were fewer and farther between. But the chatter and occasional laughter did not include the parson and his wife.

Only the Government House clerk, Jonathan Kincaid, stopped to say more than good day. He spoke slowly, choosing his words carefully, his sharp eyes hinting that there were many things he left unsaid.

"An excellent sermon, sir." He put out his hand and Ian took it.

"Why, thank you!" Ian sounded truly grateful.

"You had an audience at least of one. I listened."

"Oh, I'm sure . . ." But Ian did not sound at all sure. Then he hastily added, "Words don't matter, really. It's the . . . coming together."

"And the collection plate." Jonathan's eyes twinkled.

"Yes," Ian admitted with a twist of a smile.

"You almost had a new member this morning." Jonathan was looking at Lilias now.

"Oh?"

"Standing wistfully outside a window."

Lilias could feel herself blushing but she looked the other way.

"You saw the goat, didn't you, Mrs. Everett?"

"I think it would be quite all right for you to

call me Lilias, Jonathan. After all, we are all good friends. Isn't that true, Ian?"

"That is true," Ian agreed. "You are a good friend, Jonathan. You say you saw a goat wanting to come in to the service?"

"Watching and listening. He looked almost human."

"He looked like Governor Appleby," Lilias added quietly.

Ian shook his head. "Now, Lilias, my dear . . ." but Jonathan laughed.

The laugh made some of the parishioners in the group below turn and look back at the trio at the church entrance.

Ian said quickly, "Would you care to stop for some tea, Jonathan? Or are you in a hurry to keep a dinner engagement in town?"

"No engagement. Delighted."

Ian stopped long enough to close the church doors.

"I should not wish my four-footed would-be member of the congregation to come in when the church is empty. This is not a Catholic church."

"Do you suppose the Catholics welcome goats?" Jonathan asked.

"They welcome . . ." Ian frowned. "Never mind. Come along."

The walk around the church and up the rocky path to the house was not long but the sun was directly overhead and mercilessly bright. The wild vines and bushes that bordered the path hung limply, the stones hot through the soles of her shoes. Lilias wished she could take off that ornate brown dress, and her hoops, and fling on a loose dressing gown. But that would have to wait until after Jonathan left.

Their small parlor was blinding dark after the sunshine. It had as thick walls as the church, but small, high windows with heavy wooden shutters. The shade kept it cool but nothing could make it cozy. Nothing could be cozy in this climate, Lilias thought, remembering Aunt Rachel's house in London—the embossed wallpaper, the leather-covered chairs with their sturdy carved legs, the round table with its embroidered floor-length covering. And the hearth, and the chandelier shining against the high white ceiling.

Here the furniture was crude, island-made of the local mahogany, serviceable but uncomfortable. On the one table—this was their dining room as well—Aunt Rachel's silver service, a wedding present, seemed less like a touch of home than something incongruous. The sea air and the constant dampness made it necessary for Lilias to polish it every few days, and already her precious supply of silver polish was running low.

She excused herself and went into the one bedroom to the wash stand, rinsed her hands, removed her scarf, put cologne on her forehead and temples. Already her soft brown hair was limp and stringy. She brushed it back, frowning down into the small mirror atop what passed for a dressing stand.

Be happy that Jonathan came for tea. Dear Jonathan, he is the only person on this island who knows how much I long for England. Because he longs for it, too.

She went back into the parlor and lifted the lid to the silver tea pot. Zula had remembered to pour the boiling water on the tea leaves but of course much too early.

"It will be strong, I am afraid," she warned her guest.

"I like . . . strong drink."

As Lilias sat down to preside over the tea table she again thought of England, and of the simple pleasures she had left behind. Scones. The thought of little things like scones could almost bring tears to her eyes. Scones, for example, instead of Zula's idea of cookies...

She handed Jonathan his cup of tea.

"Was there a post this week?" she asked him.

"There was. At least what was news three months ago. Trouble in Scotland. Less trouble in Ireland since the French quit helping the Irish Catholics. There is strife between the king and parliament. If you can call that news. The back of the war with France was broken by Russell's victory at La Hogue. But here, of course, we're still at war with France."

Ian said thoughtfully, "Yet what is decided

in some European palace can reach across the sea to us."

Jonathan nodded. "We can't be sure, even now, that we are still a British island."

Lilias sighed. "Oh, don't talk about it, please. It frightens me. Tell me, did you get any news of the theater? Is it still flourishing under that Dutchman and his wife?"

Ian smiled. "I doubt that their royal highnesses would appreciate your nomenclature. Have you forgotten already the simple straightforward English names of William and Mary?"

"The theater lives," Jonathan told her. "Dryden is still writing."

"I miss it." The Globe. Drury Lane. All of them. Aunt Rachel had loved the theater. It was not just the dramas Lilias loved, but the going. Dressing up and sitting in a box and looking around at the audience. The clapping and the cheering.

"I miss it, too." Jonathan's eyes met hers and for once there was no sparkle in his. For a flash of a second they shared a mutual homesickness.

Then Ian swallowed his cup of tea with a gulp, put down the cup and got to his feet. He stood looking out of the window that faced the hillside down to the sea. He spoke without turning, as if he were talking to himself.

"There is drama in real life, too."

"You're right." The twinkle came back into Jonathan's eyes. "Even here on Cabra."

"I don't believe it!" Then Lilias, looking at Jonathan, did believe it. "Go on," she said. "What is the local gossip this week?"

"Gossip?" Ian repeated the word, but he did not turn.

"It's nasty, Ian," Jonathan warned. "It's nasty, but it's rather amusing."

Lilias leaned forward eagerly. "Go on!"

"It concerns Mrs. Rowena Gresham."

"Not the great Mrs. Gresham!"

"Great?" Jonathan chuckled. "Well, if the story is true, she is rather great."

"Go on," Lilias repeated.

"Well, you have heard of cattle thievery going on on Cabra."

Ian had turned at last. "Rumors."

"Some true," Jonathan retorted. "At any rate, the Gresham land does slope down toward the caves."

"Yes."

"And buccaneers are known to have used those caves."

"So they say."

"It's quite true. Pieces of loot have been found there. And nearby, a *boucan*."

"So far you have no story." Ian smiled. "Only rumors."

"My story may be a rumor, too. But, all the same, it is amusing in a gruesome way."

"Then tell it!" Ian snapped.

"It seems that Mrs. Gresham saw these men

attempting to steal her cattle, and disarmed them by inviting them to tea."

"No!" Lilias gasped. "She invited pirates to tea?"

"She did. And they accepted. A half a dozen or so of them. Later, when the ship sailed away, those men's bodies were found on the beach."

"What!"

"It was strong tea. Stronger than this." Jonathan indicated his cup. "Strong enough to cover the taste of poison."

Ian said, very softly, "How cruel."

"Pirates are cruel," Jonathan reminded him.

"Cruelty is not the answer to cruelty," Ian said shortly. "Theft of a few cattle is not half the crime of sheer, premeditated murder of one's fellow men."

Lilias wondered if the story could be true. Mrs. Gresham was a formidable lady, but she did not seem the sort who would stoop to poisoning. Lilias remembered the last time they were at Government House at a reception—Mrs. Gresham standing to one side, her nose held high as she surveyed the crowd, her eyes deftly avoiding her husband. Roderick Gresham had moved from one lady to another, bowing over their hands in true cavalier fashion, murmuring compliments. When he paused in front of Lilias a shiver of excitement had run up her spine. He had said nothing to her beyond "Mrs. Everett," bowing his head slightly, and then moving on. But the way he had looked at her!

"Does Mr. Gresham know?" she asked aloud.

Jonathan glanced at her. "I have no idea. It is not the sort of question one asks a person like Roderick Gresham."

"Of course not," she quickly agreed.

Ian crossed the room, picked up his cup and held it out toward her. "Is the tea still hot?" he asked. He wanted to change the subject, of course. He hated speaking ill of anyone. He really believed in "love thy neighbor" and he hated gossip.

"Pirates are a menace," Jonathan was saying. "But there should be other means of taking care of them besides poisoned tea. Besides, it was a foolish thing for the lady to have done. The rest of the crew might see fit to take revenge. There is loyalty, you know, even among thieves."

Lilias shivered. She caught Ian's eye.

"Let's forget about your story, Jonathan." Ian's voice was quiet, but firm. "I think it is frightening Lilias."

"Oh, no!" she said quickly. He was always protecting her, treating her as if she were a delicate child. She was thinking that for the first time she had found something about Rowena Gresham to admire. *I wish I were brave enough to invite pirates to tea and poison them.* She pictured Mrs. Gresham telling her husband what she had done and Roderick Gresham being proud of his wife.

Jonathan had brought out his pipe. "May I?"

"Of course." Lilias found him the little bowl she kept for him in the corner cupboard.

Tea time slipped back into the channel that Ian preferred. Man talk, about the sugar crop, the possibilities of a hurricane, runaway slaves who must be replaced somehow. She must play the role of the good wife and listen, not comment.

After awhile she got to her feet, quietly, unnoticed, and went over to the window, leaned on the sill and let the flower-scented breeze sweep over her.

Silence. Complete silence, but for the swish of the wind in the trees, the occasional voice of a bird, the far away but steady sound of the surf against the rocks that bordered the channel.

Behind her now she could hear them speaking of war, in lower tones, so that her gentle ears would not be frightened. War. There would not be battlefields here on Cabra; the war would come from the sea. All the islands had changed hands many times—Spanish, Dutch, French, Danish flags as well as British had flown over the old fort in the harbor. Her father had been killed in a foolish war with the Dutch; her grandfather had fought the Spanish.

If the French captured Cabra, what would happen? Would they stay on? Would the

Catholic French allow Ian to stay? Would they be obliged to flee to another island, perhaps home to England?

Her's not to ask. Women did not ask such questions. Women weren't supposed to know about danger.

Love me, Ian, she thought. *Why don't you really love me? Put your arms around me and love me, make me feel like a woman, love me the way I thought you would when I married you.* Again she thought of Roderick Gresham. But no, she must not think of him in that way; that was wicked.

Far out on the water she saw a speck of movement. A pelican? No, she was too far away to be seeing a pelican. No, it was a ship, a tiny ship, way out beyond the bay, riding the waves, like a man on horseback going over the hills.

Intrigued by the only movement within her range of vision, she no longer even tried to listen to what the men were saying. She kept her eyes on the ship, watching it grow in size. Gradually it changed before her eyes, like a series of pictures being unfolded, from a child's toy to a vessel that could carry men, its array of sails braced in arcs against the wind.

Then as the ship magnified in size, she remembered: here on Cabra the war would come from the sea. She could not recognize the ship's flag. What if it were French? She turned.

"Ian, get your spyglass! Hurry!"

4.

Desmond swam away from the man in the boat, then, treading water, with only her head showing, she wondered if the man had had a good look at her before she was aware of him. She was on one side of the little bay and the boat was not coming toward her but headed directly into the shore. She watched the black boatman jump out and pull the gig up on the sand, saw Obediah coming down to meet them.

The moment the man stepped ashore and nodded to Obediah, he pointed toward her. She could see Obediah shaking his head and then all three men moved up in the direction of the distillery.

Once they had gone inside she hurriedly swam to shore, dried, and put on the shirt and pants. Then she ran into the brush and found a big eucalyptus tree, and climbed it.

She stayed there for what seemed a long time.

The black boatman came into sight first, rolling a barrel down to the boat which he in turn rowed out to the bigger boat. As he was rowing to land again, the white man came out of the distillery and down to the beach.

He stood there for a moment, looking around. Looking for her, Desmond was sure. He was a large man, well-dressed for the West Indies: plumed hat, lace scarf at his throat, high polished boots shining in the sunlight as did his russet silk suit. He had a beautiful strong body, and the confident manner that comes only with importance. Desmond was curious, but she had no intention of showing herself, for fear he knew she was a girl.

She waited in the tree until the larger boat had safely sailed away.

She took the soap and towel back to the house to give to Peg, who was bent over a wash tub at the back door.

"Who was that man?" she asked Peg, as she put the towel and soap down on a bench.

Peg didn't look up. "Dunno," she grunted. "He come to the distillery. I stay here."

Of course. Desmond had almost forgotten. Peg was a runaway slave.

"Where is Obediah?"

"In the distillery."

Desmond had not yet been there but now on impulse she decided to go over. And ask about the handsome visitor.

The distillery was on three levels, the main entrance at the top. There Buck was driving a mule around and around to turn the machinery that ground the sugar cane. It was hot in the sun but Buck was patient, alternately throwing cane into the machine and kicking or switching the mule to keep him going.

Desmond walked past him, stepped inside past the vats where the sugar cane was cooking, past the tubs where it was fermenting pungently, and down some big stone steps to a small room at the bottom, full of barrels and demijohns and bottles. There Obediah sat watching a little trickle of liquid coming out of a pipe and dropping plunk, plunk, slowly into a big tub.

Obediah looked up.

"Where have you been?" were his first words.

"Bathing in the sea."

"I know. He saw you."

"He did? I mean, he really saw me?"

"Yes. He asked who the girl was."

"What did you tell him?" She held her breath.

Obediah looked at her steadily.

"I told him he had made a mistake. That there was no girl here."

"Oh, thank you!"

"I think I made a mistake." He was looking down now, at the trickle of fresh rum. "I should have told him the truth. I've been sitting here thinking about it. You could do worse than to be found by someone like Roderick Gresham."

"Roderick Gresham? Who is he?"

"Only the richest man on Cabra."

"A nobleman?"

49

"No." Obediah smiled and shook his head. "He came here a nobody. A vagabond. He made himself a gentleman because of his money. Smart, but vulgar. I despise him. But he is a good customer. And, it is wise to be a friend of Gresham's."

"If he found me, like you said, what would he do?"

Obediah looked at her again.

"He is fond of young girls. He would buy you pretty clothes, and trinkets, he would find you a better place to live than the porch of Obediah's hut. You can't stay here forever, Desmond."

"I've only been here two nights! I never intended to stay forever. Never!"

"I know. You were tired and hurt. You needed us. I shouldn't have said what I did. But I was just thinking of you, and what's going to become of you."

"You mean you wish you'd sold me to this Mr. Gresham!" she said angrily.

"I meant no such thing. But you could have met. It's just that . . . wouldn't you like to be rich? Wouldn't you like to have someone taking care of you?"

"No!" She stood there, legs apart, hands on her hips, tossing back her hair. "I want to be rich, yes. I want that more than anything else in the world. But I want to get the riches as a man would, by myself. I won't be paid for

. . . for my body. I'd rather be back with the pirates!"

"Pirates!" Old Obediah sat up straighter, his mouth falling open. He swallowed, then he said, "You mean, when you were a cabin boy you were on a pirate ship?"

"Yes."

"How could you have fooled them?"

"You've only seen me since the accident, as you called it. I've been different these last two days. But before that, before they found out I wasn't a boy, I was doing very well. I was learning how to do all sorts of things and I was all ready to go with them when they took a ship. And then an officer—oh, that man!—he pretended he was teaching me how to sword fight. But he had guessed my secret, and he ripped open my shirt."

Obediah got up and studied the height of the liquid in the rum vat. He said, "You admitted you were scared stiff when you jumped ship. I can see why, now. They would have raped you, every last one of the rotten devils. And then probably killed you."

"Just because I'm a girl."

"Just because you're a girl."

"I hate men!" she cried vehemently.

"You hate me?"

"Oh, no, Obediah, no!" She reached out to take his hand.

"You see, all men are not wicked."

There was a clink on the stone steps and they

51

both turned. Little Charlie was coming down, slowly, step by step.

Obediah jumped to his feet.

"Charlie, be careful! You know you're not supposed to come down here."

"How old is Charlie?" Desmond asked.

"Three."

"He's your child." She said it as a matter of fact.

"Yes."

"And Buck?"

"He came with Peg. They ran away together from Antigua. Her name's not really Peg, you know. I just called her that. My mom, back in England, she was Peg. Peg's like her. She's so . . . good." He turned back to the boy. "Well, Charlie, what is it? Why did you come down here where you don't belong?"

Charlie took a deep breath. He frowned. Finally he said, "Dinner. Mammy said . . . dinner."

Obediah went over and swept the little boy up in the air. "Come on, Desmond. It's time for dinner."

He climbed the steps and Desmond followed. Just as they reached the out of doors and emerged into the glare of the midday sun, Obediah put the child down and turned to Desmond.

"Don't think you have to run off again, because of what I said. I'll try and find a home for you. What can you do, besides swing a cutlass and climb a rigging? Can you cook?"

Desmond shook her head.

"Peg can teach you."

Desmond thought: he *is* kind; he *is* good; he wants to help me. But I'll never be happy trying to be somebody's servant. Never in the world.

For a few days Desmond became Peg's pupil. She worked hard at domesticity, out of gratitude to Obediah and Peg, but she hated the chores. Finally one morning she ran out to the distillery and confronted Obediah.

"It's no use, I can't do it. I won't do it. Let me help here. Look, I can drive the mule, I can carry wood, I can do a man's job."

"So you want to go on pretending," he said flatly.

"Yes!"

"You're a fool. But have it your own way. Get to work."

"What shall I do?"

"Start filling these bottles . . . boy." Obediah grinned. "And don't spill."

"And if anybody comes to buy rum, you won't tell them?"

"I'll let them guess. You're on your own, little fool."

She went to work.

Occasionally people came to buy rum. No one like Roderick Gresham, of course. Most of them were servants, white or black, who paid little attention to Obediah's new help. She rolled barrels down to the waterfront, or carried bottles, wishing she could sail away herself, to another waterfront, to another job at sea.

After each visitor Obediah would explain for whom the rum was intended, names of people in Edwardsville that meant nothing to Desmond.

And then one afternoon a schooner appeared on the horizon, in full sail. They all stood admiring it, watching it, the way people in lonely spots will watch anything that moves. To their surprise, the ship came closer and closer, dropped anchor, and they could see men climbing into a small boat.

Obediah frowned and shook his head. "I don't like it."

"What ship is it?" Desmond asked. "Do you know it?"

"No. But from the looks of it, I suspect it might be some of your friends."

"My friends?"

"Sometimes pirates come here. Not to buy; to take. One gang usually operates out of Cabra. They camp out near the Cabra Caves; they've been known to use the caves. They've also been known to come here to take rum, and I'm helpless to stop them. The authorities in Edwardsville—the governor himself—know about it, but pretend they don't. To their own ad-

54

vantage, of course. They get paid off with a handful of doubloons every now and then."

The small boat was coming closer. There were half a dozen men aboard. Soon the telltale bandannas and hats and sashes were clearly visible.

"Peg, take Charlie in the house and stay there. You, too, Buck. Desmond . . ."

She was staring at the approaching boat, excited, apprehensive, curious.

"Desmond, go cut some of those dead branches."

Reluctantly she went for the cutlass and moved into the bush near the distillery, out of sight, but not out of hearing.

She heard the men's feet on the path; she heard Obediah say, "So it's you, Barnes." And then, after no reply, "You have a new ship."

"Aye, we do. Is she not a beauty? The *Poinciana*. A Spanish prize."

"I suppose I should offer congratulations?"

The other man roared with laughter. "That's right, Obie. Congratulations and two barrels of rum."

"You're a thief and a braggart."

"I know it."

"Take your rum, and go!"

"Obie, I shouldn't want to hurt you. You're a good fellow and you make good rum."

"Let go of me, Ned Barnes!"

Desmond did not hesitate. Although she could not see, she heard every word. Cutlass in hand, she ran out of the woods and straight to the entrance of the distillery.

"Stop it!"

The man called Barnes turned as she cried out. His voice had given no hint of his appearance. He was rangy and ugly, his twisted nose and wet loose lips and narrow eyes made uglier by the scars on his face and one missing ear.

She held the cutlass high. "You leave Obediah alone! Like he says, take your rum and go!"

The man let go of Obediah but he kept his eyes on Desmond.

"I see you have new help."

"Yes," Obediah said under his breath.

"A healthy lad."

"Yes."

"We could use him aboard."

Slowly Desmond lowered her cutlass. She could feel herself trembling under the man's stare. Two years ago it had seemed easy to pretend she was a boy. But it was different now. How long would Obie's old shirt disguise her growing breasts? For they were still growing, as were her buttocks. She glanced at Obediah, wondering if he would break his promise and tell them about her. But if he did . . . she caught her breath in panic. If he did, they might take her anyhow, as they were taking the rum!

Obediah spoke very slowly, as if he were

having difficulty in remembering to say *he* instead of *she*.

"Desmond is a good worker. I need . . . him."

"Desmond, eh," Barnes said. "That's your name?"

"Desmond Duval."

"French? Martinique? Guadeloupe?"

"Barbados."

"You're quite a way from home. You've shipped out before? You've sailed?"

"Yes, sir." Reluctantly.

"And you can handle a cutlass."

She nodded.

"I need Desmond here, Barnes."

"Do you really? You got along very well, before, it seems to me. And we are shorthanded. We've lost a lot of our men."

"Capturing your prize boat."

"Before that. By a vixen on Cabra."

"Vixen?"

"Who's known as a lady. Mrs. Roderick Gresham."

Desmond and Obediah looked at each other. She remembered that name. The richest planter on the island. The man who had seen her naked in the water.

"What about Mrs. Gresham?" Obediah finally asked.

"How about a drink of rum?" Barnes answered. "We are all thirsty."

57

"Desmond, will you—" Obediah started to say, but Barnes interrupted.

"You fetch it, Obie. I'd rather keep my eye on this young man."

His homely appearance was not quite so repulsive now. He was nothing like Batham on the *Lady May.* There were class distinctions among pirates, she knew, but they still were pirates, she reminded herself, capable of anything. As Obediah went into the distillery, the pirate asked:

"What kind of ship were you on?"

When she told him, he nodded. Then he asked, abruptly, "Why did you leave the ship?"

"They were cruel to me. I did my work well, but they were cruel."

"I see."

Obediah had come back with a bottle and a basket full of coconut shells. After the rum had been passed around Obediah said, again, "What about Mrs. Gresham? You didn't finish your story."

Barnes had been looking at Desmond, very thoughtfully. He kept on looking at her as he answered.

"Some of my men were near Gresham's land. They were rounding up a few stray cattle. Mrs. Gresham encountered them, invited them to tea. Like fools they went. She poisoned them. Some day we shall repay that woman, in full."

"Stealing is wrong," Obediah said after a moment.

"Obie, this is a cruel world. It's a fight just to live. There are no more rules of conduct for anyone, on sea or on land, or even in the high places. It's every man for himself. Isn't that true, Desmond?"

She said, "Yes, sir," again—not that she liked what he had been saying, but because she felt in her heart that it was true, that it was the way of the world. Besides, Barnes was the kind of man one obeyed, unthinking.

Barnes drained his cup of rum.

"Obie, we want two barrels of rum. And the boy."

He had his hands on his hips now, next to the pistols hanging from his belt. His men had finished their rum and stood in a half-circle behind him, like guards surrounding a nobleman. Resistance would be impossible.

"You will be good to Desmond?" Obediah asked.

"Good? We shall be fair. You know, Dragon is always fair."

"Yes."

"If the boy does his work, he will come to no harm." He turned to his men. "Fetch the barrels."

As the men ran into the distillery, Obediah looked across at her. She could tell by the expression on his face that he must be feeling the same way she did, that he was resisting the impulse to put his arms around her. She wanted to put her arms around his neck and thank him for all his kindnesses.

She turned to Barnes. "Does your ship come to Cabra often?"

He actually smiled. "Often," he said. "It is one of our most regular calls."

She turned back to Obediah. "Then I'll come and see you. I promise!"

There were tears in the old man's eyes, but he said nothing.

She would have liked to have gone to the house and told Peg and Buck and little Charlie goodby, but she knew that was not wise. Obediah liked to keep them hidden, Peg and little Charlie in particular. Nor did she dare send the message by Obediah.

When the men emerged with the two barrels and started down toward the beach, Barnes indicated that she should follow. Obediah reached out and took her hand, shook it solemnly, with a touch that was warm and firm. She turned around and hurried after the men, shaking tears from her eyes. *I must not show my fear*, she determined. *I must not look weak. Just be quiet, obedient, do my work, like he says, and everything will be all right.*

Barnes, of course, was the last to get into the small boat and the only space left was beside her. She looked back at Obediah, standing there at the entrance to the distillery, waving, and she waved back.

"You're rather fond of the old boy, aren't you?"

Desmond blinked back her tears, lifted her chin. "Yes," she said softly. "He's been a friend."

"The ship you were on came here for rum."

"No, I swam ashore."

"And he took you in."

"Yes."

She did not want to remember that night. She must not think of what happened on the *Lady May*, nor be afraid that it would happen again. She prayed that the heavy, over-large shirt that had been Obie's would disguise her.

One of the men asked, "Ned, where are we headed?"

Barnes answered, "The caves."

She had assumed that Barnes was the captain. But the man had used his first name.

She asked, "Who is Dragon?"

"Our captain," Barnes said. "He's coming aboard tonight."

"I thought you were the captain."

"I'm just in charge. I'm the quartermaster. Dragon does not always sail with us."

Obediah's little shack and the stone walls of the distillery had been absorbed by the green bank of the island, by the time they reached the *Poinciana*. It was a beautiful ship, its figurehead a buxom black-haired female. It was flamboyantly painted in Spanish fashion, red and yellow. It showed no Spanish flag now but the crew's own skull and crossbones and bottle. A rope ladder hung over the side, waiting, and Barnes told her to climb up first. She was proud to display her agility at ladders; her pride helped cover her nervousness at the audience above her.

"New hand, eh, Ned?" one asked as the boatswain piped them aboard.

The barrels of rum brought aboard, they were ready to sail. The quartermaster said, "Up the rigging, lad, and free that main halyard."

Desmond looked up. The lines were heavier than those she had dealt with before, but it was up to her to climb up and do it.

She scrambled agilely up the ratlines, but by the time she reached her position, the wind had risen and the masts were swaying, and it was with great difficulty that she freed the halyard that was jammed in the block. But as she slid down the halyard a cheer came up from the deck.

Soon the sails began to draw and the *Poinciana* set forth.

The deck was aslant when she reached it and the wind had brought with it rain that beat across the ship. They were out in the channel now; the storm had obliterated the shore. She skidded across and hurried inside the galley.

An old man was bent over the stove. He looked up as she came in. His sleeves were rolled up, his old arms were covered with tattoos of sea serpents.

"So you're the new one. How old are you, anyhow?"

"Sixteen."

"You're kind of scrawny."

"Yes, sir," she agreed.

"Forget the sir. You can call me Bombo."

"Bombo!" It was a drink for children, of lime juice and sugar.

"I'm the only bloke aboard what don't drink rum."

"Oh, I don't like rum, either."

"You're too young, I guess, and I'm too old."

Desmond stood in the door to watch the sun begin to sink. The rain had passed and the wind died down as they rounded a nubby peninsula and turned shoreward. The ship was now a black skeleton moving across rose-colored waters.

"Do we stop somewhere tonight?" she asked Bombo.

"No. We're just picking up Dragon. We'll be sailing tonight. Maybe working by dawn."

Working. Attacking a ship. What would her role be? Would they put her high on the mast as a lookout? Would they make her stand guard over some loot already hidden on the vessel? Or would they let her, at long last, go with them? *Don't expect too much*, she told herself, *after all, you just got on board. They don't know you well enough to trust you very far.*

The ship stopped, and a boat was put out in the dark with one man at the oars. They waited in the silence and the darkness, then the shish-shish of the oars against the waves as the boat rejoined them.

She heard the small boat pull against the ship and hurried aft to get a better look.

In the flash of a moment a head appeared over the side of the ship and a slender man leapt aboard. He moved quickly and Desmond followed.

She had her first good look at Dragon when she reached the door to the great cabin. He was in earnest conversation with Ned Barnes.

Then he turned his head. It was a surprisingly boyish face, round and smooth, yet even in the lantern light she could see the gray at the temples. His face was mild, but his voice when he spoke was resonant with authority, although all he said, staring at her, was:

"Who is this?"

5.

Ian had hastily dispersed Lilias' fear about the strange ship she had seen down in the channel. One swift look through his brass spyglass and he said, "It is not French, my sweet, nor even Spanish. Merely a Dutch trader. No need for alarm with a Dutch king. There is not much danger of our being at war with Holland."

Jonathan, who had risen to tap the ashes from his pipe and to take his farewell, said in the quietest of voices, "It could be a pirate ship, flying under a false flag."

"You brood on pirates," Ian said lightly, putting his hand on his wife's shoulder, in a comforting gesture.

Even if it were a French ship, she thought, *he wouldn't tell me. He somehow has the notion that I will be safer in ignorance than with knowledge.*

"At any rate, I shall soon find out," Jonathan said. "I must wend my way down to the harbor and meet that ship. It may bring mail. In times like these I am afraid I cannot always remember the sabbath, parson."

"I understand."

"Should there be anything of import, I should be obliged to disturb his excellency from his Sunday afternoon snooze."

"I hope there will be no bad news," Lilias said.

Jonathan shrugged. "I shall hope for no news. You know what they say about no news." He smiled. "At any rate, do not trouble yourself. And thank you so much, for the tea."

"You are always welcome, Jonathan," Lilias told him.

When the door was closed on their guest, she said, "You were rather rude to Jonathan."

"Was I? I didn't think so. He is an outspoken man himself."

"He's very intelligent. I like him."

"I know you do."

Lilias cocked her head. "You're jealous, perhaps?" she teased.

"Oh, no. Of course not."

Was he incapable of jealousy? Did he take her for granted? Was it the whole idea of jealousy he was spurning, because he was so sure of her, or was it the idea of being jealous of Jonathan Kincaid? She hoped it was the latter case. She would like to have Ian jealous; she would like to arouse him to real fervor.

"It is time that I went back to the chapel," he said. "I must tidy up my papers so that Zula may dust and sweep. And there is the collection plate, waiting. I must count, and lock up our wealth in the chest. I'll see you at dinner."

Dinner was midafternoon on Sunday, a good two hours away, Lilias sighed.

Ian had started to leave the room. He turned back.

"Oh, yes, I forgot to give you this. Mrs. Gresham handed it to me as they were leaving church. I imagine it is some sort of invitation."

He handed her a sealed envelope.

She began to open it as he walked away, and sat down to read Mrs. Gresham's impeccable stilted hand.

It *was* an invitation to a reception honoring the Governor and his wife, and the Governor's brother, who was to be visiting, from Jamaica.

There were few social occasions on Cabra and Lilias snatched happily at any invitation—anything besides sitting alone in this little house, reading and re-reading the few books she had brought with her, or playing audience while Ian rehearsed his sermons aloud, or mending sheets and pillow cases. She welcomed any chance to get out in the world where for a little while, in spite of the climate and the limited choice of conversationalists, she could pretend she was at a soiree in London. And there was always plenteous food, generously served, and bowls of rum punch. And the pleasant murmur of inconsequential conversation. And Roderick Gresham would be there . . .

It was also a chance to dress.

In what? So much of her limited trousseau had been unsuitable for the West Indies. Aunt

Rachel had not known what it would be like out here. There was that sprigged white dimity, intended for a "garden frock," so cool and agreeably comfortable that she had worn it much too often. What could she do to change it?

She went into the bedroom and began whisking through the commode. Here, that pink silk petticoat she had torn, walking no farther than from the chapel to the house. She could abandon it as a petticoat; she could cut off a swath and make a sash, and another swath to make a trim for her old straw bonnet.

Pink. Her color, Aunt Rachel had always said.

The morning of the day of the reception Ian came back from a trip to town and told her he would be going off island that afternoon.

"Oh, Ian, no! No, not today! Today is the Gresham reception."

"I know."

"But, Ian, can't those off island people wait another day?" she pleaded.

"I've put it off too long, my dear. Besides, that family on Pollino are ill. They need food and medicine. The doctor got word of it."

"They're fools to live over there with the Indians!"

"They're not with the Caribs, Lilias. They're on the other side of Pollino. And it's not only that family. There are other islands, other poor. It will only be for a few days."

68

"I still think you could wait until tomorrow." She was cross, thinking of the work she had done on that dress and bonnet, thinking of the party.

"Don't pout, my dear. You will not miss the reception."

She looked up. How could she not? She never went anywhere when Ian was away.

"I spoke to the Greshams. I explained. And I asked Jonathan to fetch you. Now, will you wipe off that frown?"

"Oh, Ian!" She threw her arms around his neck.

He held her for a moment, patting her shoulder. "You're such a child," he said softly.

I'm not, I'm not! she wanted to cry out. *Treat me like a woman and I'll be a woman.* And yet she knew how she appeared to him, making such a fuss over one party, not remembering that as a minister's wife she must expect to play second fiddle to the church.

When he released her she said, "Thank you, Ian, for arranging everything," with a dignity she hoped he would recognize and appreciate.

"Have a good time. And don't look too beautiful . . . when I am not with you."

When Jonathan arrived to pick her up that evening she knew she had done her best to make herself beautiful, because his eyebrows went up a little at the first sight of her, although he said nothing. He seemed a bit shy,

69

as if he felt awkward in the role of the escort of the parson's wife.

She tried to put him at ease by asking about the Dutch ship he had headed for when he left after Sunday tea.

"Was there a post? Is there any news from home?"

He shook his head. "Nothing of any moment. My sister has had the pox but she is recovering nicely with only a minimal of pockmarks."

"Thank God for that."

Jonathan had a small two-seater carriage, drawn by a donkey. The road down the mountain to the coast, and around to the village of Edwardsville seemed rougher than usual, and of course windier, because of that decorated bonnet, which she clutched firmly in her hand all the way.

They came into town, drove past the handful of houses with their meager lights, and then up the hill on the other side to the Gresham estate. The Greshams were not far from town, but their land was extensive, running downhill toward the Cabra Caves. The sun had set not long before, and the stars were just beginning to come out. The air was scented with sea and flower, and it was a night that cried out for romance.

The Gresham house was big, even bigger than Government House, which dominated the town. It was built of stone, as many of the houses were; only the poor blacks lived in wooden shacks. There were stone columns on the portico—a big porch with a long flight of stairs running down to the road. Tonight the whole building was ablaze with candles, so that riding up to it even the road seemed more brightly lit. It was like approaching a palace, Lilias thought.

There should have been music. There should have been dancing. Dancing. Of course Ian never danced; it was against his Protestant religion. Protest, protest, always protest against the gaiety of the world.

Jonathan helped her from the carriage, and one of the slaves took the carriage away. Jonathan took her arm and with her free hand she lifted her full skirt just enough to clear the stone steps as they climbed.

Receptions had a pattern. First, the receiving line: the Greshams, the Governor and his wife, the Governor's brother, (looking less like a goat than a sick sheep) other dignitaries—not the preacher, not the doctor—but the town lawyer, the tax collector, and so on, and then the merchants and their wives. Lilias and Jonathan passed along the line and took their places at the end, while the rest of the guests passed by. Then, the formalities over, everyone was free to walk about the grand hall and take their places near windows, or close to the big revolving fans the slaves were kept busy turning, to wait until the signal that refreshments would be served.

Soon after this bit of secondary ritual, one of

71

the servants came over and spoke to Jonathan. The governor wanted to see him. Jonathan excused himself and left Lilias alone by one of the deep-set windows looking down on the bay.

She was thinking that the first person to approach her would be someone offering sympathy for her being without her husband that evening, to praise him for his good work among the poor, his trips to the outer islands to visit his far flung flock. To her surprise it was her host, who had been circling among the guests, bowing over ladies' hands, who moved swiftly and directly to her side.

He bowed slightly. "Mrs. Everett?"

She extended her hand.

He held it for a moment, her palm turned downward to his. He looked down at it and then slowly, deliberately, and not in the least casually, he lifted it to his lips.

They were hot, clinging. It was only a moment's touch, but it was not the butterfly flicker of before, it was not the way one kissed the hand of the parson's wife. And before he let go of her hand he was saying, "Mrs. Everett, you look charming this evening."

He had kissed her hand on other occasions, in the same way, but had said nothing. Tonight's compliment engendered a reply.

"Thank you," she said. Then she added, "Is that so unusual?"

His eyes were big and black, like his long

Cavalier-style curls, his mustache, his trim beard. His eyes widened now, as if amused.

"Not at all unusual." His voice was low. "I've been admiring you, from a respectful distance, ever since you set foot on this desolate island."

"Why, thank you," she said again. It seemed like a foolish response, but no other words came to her lips. Then, just to say something, anything, she went on. "I am surprised to hear you call Cabra desolate. It's so verdant. Everything grows profusely. Like your sugar cane."

"I wasn't thinking of that." His eyes were growing intense. "I was thinking of women. There is a dearth of beautiful women."

"Oh, I think you can find plenty of women . . ."

She had spoken hastily, unthinkingly; her words had come out like an insult. Gresham's affairs were part of the island gossip. But he only threw back his head and laughed.

"Plenty of women, yes. But beautiful ones . . ." His eyes swept over her face, lingered at the top of her bodice. "Beautiful ones," he repeated, "are rare."

This time she did not try to answer. She fluttered her fan, half-obscuring her face. She was remembering Ian's words about not looking too beautiful, and wondering if she had made a mistake touching up her dress and hat, but then she realized Gresham was not looking at her clothes, but at her. He had not spoken admiringly about her clothes. In fact she felt as if he were mentally stripping them from her.

73

"You're lonesome, aren't you, Mrs. Everett? You're lonesome and bored with Cabra. You belong in another world."

She caught her breath and bit her lip. She murmured, "I don't know what you're talking about."

"Of course you do. Some time, somewhere, you will tell me all about it. You are dying to tell me all about it, right at this moment."

She turned her head and looked around her, wishing Jonathan would come back. Jonathan, or anybody, so that Mr. Gresham would stop talking this way, so that she could compose herself and her feelings.

"Are you having a pleasant time, Mrs. Everett?"

Lilias jumped.

Mrs. Gresham was standing beside her now. Usually the woman circulated constantly among her guests, but in counter circle to her husband. Now she was beside him and it was strange, but they almost resembled one another. Both were tall and big-boned, both dark, but Rowena Gresham's face held none of the charm of her husband's. Hers was proud, self-righteous. *I am always right* was in the very set of her jaw.

Lilias turned toward her hostess, somehow feeling guilty. Guilty of what?

"I am sorry that reverend was not able to be with us this evening," Mrs. Gresham went on.

"He is sorry, too. He sent his regrets."

"I know. He gave them to me, in person. But as he said, duty comes first."

"I know."

"How long will he be away?"

"A few days."

"Aren't you afraid, way up in the hills, alone?"

"No. I have the servants."

She could practically feel Gresham's eyes upon her. He had guessed so correctly about so many things, in just a few moments. He probably guessed that she was not telling the truth, that she was afraid when she was alone.

"Of course." Mrs. Gresham glanced the other way for a moment, before she said, "Refreshments are being served."

Guests were lining up at the long table along the end of the room. Lilias was glad to join them.

Roderick Gresham did not come near her for the rest of the evening. Jonathan came back, at first preoccupied with whatever Governor Appleby had told him. They were joined by some of the others, but conversation swirled around Lilias with little meaning. She was still thinking of Gresham, the way he had kissed her hand, the way he had looked at her, the things he had said. It was an obsession she found hard to shake off.

They were riding home along the black star-lit road when Jonathan said, "You're very quiet, Lilias. Didn't you enjoy yourself this evening?"

"Oh, yes. Yes, I did," she said quickly. "It was good of you to take me."

"I saw our host palavering over you."

"Palavering?"

"You know what I mean. He's such a lady's man."

"He was just . . ." But she did not know how to explain, had she wanted to, the way Gresham had made her feel.

"I don't trust him. He's half-French, you know."

"No, I did not know. But what does . . ."

"Don't be stupid, Lilias. He pretends not to be, but he is a traitor. Or would be, if he had the opportunity. He's always sniffing around Government House, pumping me."

"Really?" She did not care about that; it did not matter. She had enjoyed herself that evening. It hadn't been the food, nor the sip of rum punch, it had been those few moments with a man looking at her as Roderick Gresham had; she had come alive for the first time in months. Some time, some where, he had said, she would tell him all about her feelings. How? Where? When? It was impossible. She was a married woman. Besides, it was a small island, a small world of people in which each one had his or her place. It could only be a dream, a perhaps, a maybe . . .

"Be careful, Lilias," Jonathan said, not looking at her, but directly ahead up the dark road, now winding into the crouching hills. "You are so innocent. Such a child."

"I am not a child!" she cried out angrily, as she had wanted to cry to Ian that morning, so suddenly that Jonathan turned and tried to look into her face, even in the dark. "I'm a grown woman, a grown woman, alive and real. I have a brain and I have feelings, too. I don't want to go on forever and forever being sheltered and protected, up on a shelf like a piece of fragile china. I'm sick of it. I tell you, I'm sick of it!"

She burst into tears.

Slowly Jonathan pulled the donkey to a halt.

He put his arms around her and held her close. She clung to him, her breasts firm against him. It was not a fatherly hug he was giving her, not at all, although despite what she had said she had spoken like a child.

Quickly he released her, pulled a kerchief from his pocket and wiped away her tears.

"I'd better get you home, Lilias."

The church, and then her house, and even the little shack where Zula and the yard man lived, were only dark little blobs under the stars.

Jonathan helped her from the carriage, took her arm as they crossed to the door, opened it, and went inside with her to find a candle.

"Your maid should have left a light," Jonathan said.

"She's not supposed to—it might start a fire."

"She could have waited up for you."

"I told her to go to bed. She works hard; she's very tired by evening."

There was a candle in a holder on the little table beside the door. Jonathan lit it and then looked at her. She knew she was still flushed from her angry outburst, but she tried to compose her face.

"Thank you Jonathan, for taking me there tonight. And for bringing me home."

"You'll be all right?"

"Of course I'll be all right. Ian has been away before. And of course I'll bolt the door."

"Stone walls do not a prison make, nor iron bars a cage."

"Lovelace!"

"Lovelace. More than a poem. A warning."

"Good night, Jonathan," she said quickly.

"Good night." But he did not move. He said, "You are right, Lilias, you are not a child. That is all the more reason for me to say . . . be careful."

And with that he turned on his heel, walked out the front door, and banged it shut behind him.

Lilias stood there for a moment, listening to his footsteps and then to the carriage and donkey clop-clopping away, before she moved slowly to the door and swung the bolt.

She was not in the least bit sleepy. She never had felt more wide awake in all her life.

Her whole world had shrunk to the space of

78

light around that small candle. And yet, at the same time, it expanded to a new width, a new depth. It was as if she had discovered a new power within herself, a power she had not realized before that she possessed. A power over men.

She took the candle into the bedroom, carrying the new feeling with her.

She felt so alive, so truly alive.

She undressed slowly, putting away the bonnet and letting down her hair, hanging her dress in the commode, draping her undergarments over the room's one chair. She stood naked in the candle light. She never had stood naked before Ian; she had always been carefully covered, awake or asleep. Now she looked down at her small, erect breasts, ran her hands over her hips and her thighs. She thought of Greek statues in the moonlight. But her body was warm and soft to the touch, not at all like cold marble. She thought of a man's hand touching her body, of a man's lips on her breasts.

This was nonsense. This was extending a vague dream beyond reasonable limits. She must prepare herself for bed, she must sleep, as if this had been any evening, as if she had not felt such a fire of excitement.

Slowly she put on her nightgown. It was cotton, a summer nightgown Aunt Rachel had called it, but it was much too long, too full, for the tropics. There were long sleeves with ruffles at her wrists. Certainly no covers were needed over it. She blew out her candle and lay down on the bed.

It was a long time, after much tossing and turning, that she finally fell asleep.

She was awakened by a persistent, steady, small noise. At first she did not know what it was. Finally she realized it was the front door, someone trying to switch open the bolt.

Ian. It must be Ian. Once before he had come home unexpectedly, late at night.

She did not bother to search for her dressing gown. She lit the candle, called out, "Coming!" and hurried out across the living room to the front door.

She put down the candle on the little table. Fumbling, she struggled with the bolt, which was somewhat rusted and very stiff. At last, groaning, it moved, and she was able to open the door.

"Ian, you're back!" she cried out as she swung the door wide.

It was not Ian. Even in the starlit dark she recognized the outline of Roderick Gresham's body.

6.

Desmond stood hesitant in the cabin doorway as Dragon asked Barnes who she was. She dared not turn and run, as she wanted to—that would amount to insubordination.

"I picked him up at the distillery," Barnes explained.

"Awfully young." Dragon shook his head.

"I'm sixteen, sir!"

"You don't look it." Like a challenge.

"Probably been lying about his age." Ned Barnes chuckled. "Lots of boys do, these days. But he's strong. And nimble. Climbed the rigging like a monkey. And he's sailed before. I think he'll do."

"And your name?" Dragon asked her.

"Desmond Duval."

"Desmond Duval, eh."

"Probably made that up, along with his age," Ned Barnes laughed now. "Run along, boy, we're busy. Bombo will issue you a hammock."

Desmond wanted to scream out in protest. She got as far as clenching her fists, and then she thought: she was pretending to be a boy, she must also pretend to be the kind of boy they would expect her to be. But she could not resist saying, "My name *is* Desmond Duval and I *am* sixteen!" before she turned and left the cabin doorway.

Slowly the *Poinciana* was pulling away from land and moving out into the channel. Desmond had no idea who was at the wheel, or which way they were headed.

The wind was mild and soft, too mild to fill the sails, which hung lazily against the mast. The ship moved slowly with the tide.

As she came on deck she could smell food. Bombo was dishing out pieces of dried salted beef and boiled plantain.

The meat, tough and chewy, still was food, when one was hungry enough. Its odor was nothing as delicious as it had been when it was being prepared.

She remembered when the *Lady May* had anchored off a lonely, uninhabited island, in order to smoke the meat from the cattle they recently had slaughtered. The ship surgeon had cut the beef into long strips, less than two inches thick, and powdered them with salt. While they waited the necessary twenty-four hours Desmond had helped gather wood and sticks to build the *boucan*. Under a dome-shaped hut, covered with leaves, there had been a rack for the strips of meat, after the salt had been brushed from them, and under the rack a fire had been built, a fire of green wood liberally sprinkled with the bones and skins of the animals. The pungent smoke had penetrated the meat as it "cooked."

She thought bitterly of the woman who had poisoned the men who had been after the cattle. They had to have cattle, didn't they? They had to have food! A rich woman who lived in a big house should not have minded a few men taking a few head of cattle.

This would be the crew's meal. Those two men in the cabin would have something more enticing to eat, she felt sure.

Nothing in the world was fair, she thought, as she stood in line for her tough meat and cold plantain.

Meat in one hand, plantain in the other, she squatted down next to old Bombo, who so far had seemed the friendliest of the crew. He was having great difficulty with the meat for what teeth he had left were no more than fragments.

He stopped chewing long enough to say, "You've sailed before."

Desmond, her own teeth engrossed in the meat, only nodded.

"With buccaneers?"

Another nod.

"It's a rough life but it's all I know now, and I'm too old to go ashore. I was a tailor when they captured me, because they needed a sail mender. Cooking I just learned. I'm not so good at fighting, not nowadays. But I man the galley and I mend the sails. This new ship we got, she's got good sails." He looked up at them, shadowy white against the mauve of the early evening sky. "Like birds, they look to my old eyes. Like great white birds."

He got up and went back into the galley and came back with a bottle, which he extended just as Desmond was finishing eating, slowly swallowing the last tough scrap.

"Wash it down with this, lad. Bombo from Bombo."

Desmond was grateful for the watered lime and sugar.

"So you just cook and mend sails."

"Well," old Bombo chuckled, "when they're out to take a ship, sometimes I'm in charge here," he said proudly. "Sometimes they lets me be captain."

"What about the loot? Do you get your share?"

"I get some. Not much. But more n' you, my boy. Dragon's always fair."

Desmond remembered clearly the times loot had been divided among the members of the crew of the *Lady May*, and how great her disappointment always had been. There were rules, of course. All pirates shared alike but the captain, the quartermaster, the surgeon and the pilot all got gifts from the rest of the crew. The captain got three or four extra shares; others, two. Of course the first to sight the prize ship got an extra share. But a boy, no matter how much he had contributed to the capture, only got a half a share.

In her mind's eye she still could see the treasures they had captured. The silks and satins from East India, the jewels, the bars of gold and silver—the most beautiful sight she ever had seen—and she had had to stand by and wait for her half a share. Each time she had been sure hers was lots less than half. She had been able to stuff it into one bag. Nevertheless, she had slept with it serving as a lumpy pillow under her head. She hadn't had much chance to spend it. Of course her bag had been left behind when she jumped ship.

She sighed. Some day, oh some day she would get her share. She would get enough money to go to some place, some distant island where nobody knew who she was, or where she came from. She would have beautiful clothes, women's clothes that clung to her body. She was not scrawny, as old Bombo had said. He hadn't seen the real Desmond underneath the old shirt and raggedy pants. She would be a beautiful woman, as her mother had predicted. And she would meet a man, a handsome man, as her father had been, not a dirty boy like Alan Forrester. She thought again of her mother's words—a man who would touch her in the right places. The right places. The lobes of her ears, the nape of her neck, her breasts. Before she fell asleep she would imagine the gentle touches, the stroking, his mouth on hers.

Someday. But first she must get that money. The next time a ship was captured, no matter what, no matter who tried to stop her, she would help with the fighting. She shivered a little. But she could swing a cutlass. She would have to pretend that a man was merely something in her way, or a bush that must be slashed down for firewood.

She looked over at Bombo. He had finally finished eating and was licking his fingers.

"Bombo," she asked impulsively, "where could I find a cutlass?"

"You want a cutlass?" He sounded most surprised.

"Yes. I know how to use one."

"Oh?"

"I want one so I can help. I want to earn more than a boy's share."

The old man scratched his chin. "You're sure about this?"

"Yes!"

"I prob'ly shouldn't be telling you, but there's some stashed away in the bosun's hold. Belonged to the men that vixen killed."

"I see. Where is the bosun's hold?"

"Right around the corner from the galley, next to the bosun's cabin. But Freedman—that's the bosun—ain't there now; he's with the others guzzling rum."

As Desmond got to her feet he said, "Don't tell Ned, or Dragon, that I told you."

"I promise. Thank you, Bombo."

"I like to see a young man who's got ambition." He grinned. "And guts."

If she encountered anyone she would pretend that she was exploring the ship with a boy's natural curiosity. But she encountered no one and in only a moment, even in the half-dark, she found the bosun's hold.

And more than one cutlass. She felt each one, carefully, picking one that had a handle that felt comfortable, that had the right balance for her. She had just tucked it into her belt when she heard voices and realized that above her was the fo'c'sle. Ned Barnes and Dragon were talking.

To her surprise they were not talking roughly, the way she had become used to hearing men talk. They were speaking together quietly, like old friends. Ned's voice was still rough-hewn, and a bit coarse, but Dragon's had the intonations of a gentleman.

"I am rather sorry, Ned," he was saying, "that you scuttled the old ship. This one is much too big; it is more than I think we should try to handle."

"It's a good ship."

"Yes, but it needs a bigger crew. And it is more conspicuous. Before long it will be recognized by every man in the Caribbean with a spy glass. We must paint it, Ned, paint it gray."

"But I like its paint! I like these bold Spanish colors. I'm not afraid of our being recognized. I want us to be recognized! I want everyone on every small island or cay or reef to dread the *Poinciana!*"

"Your way, Ned. Not mine."

"It should be yours."

There was a long silence before Dragon went on. His voice had taken on a certain asperity, his tone was firmer. "Ned, you seem to forget that I am the captain of this ship. It seems more and more you are assuming command."

"More and more I *am* in command."

"But you assume too much command. For instance, this new boy. What's his name?"

"Desmond. What about Desmond? He's young, strong, agile. Furthermore, he's obedient. He's been scared out of his young life and he's ready to be bossed. He's not like most of these young scalawags who run away from home with their dander up and start getting uppity in no time at all. I think I sized him up fairly well. No trouble maker. All it would take is one threat of the lash and I'm sure he'd do anything that I told him to do."

Desmond gritted her teeth in anger. So that's what he thought! That she was a coward! She'd show him a thing or two. She would not be openly rebellious, not to his face; she would simply show him what she could do. She put her hand on the cutlass.

"I don't like it." Dragon's voice was stern.

"What don't you like?"

"Your taking aboard boys as apprentices."

"Apprentice to you as well as to me, Dragon, old boy."

Another silence.

"Dragon, you should not be ashamed of this way of life. It is a decent way of life. A man has to live, a man has to fight, in order to live. What's different about warring for yourself, your rights, your livelihood—and fighting for some blasted king? We gentlemen of fortune know we risk swinging, but we eat and drink well, we have our flings. The stakes are high but the gamble's worth it. Pounds instead of farthings in your pockets."

Dragon sighed. "We've talked about this before, Ned, many times. You know how I feel."

"But you go on with it."

"You know why. Because you are my friend."

"Because you owe your life to me. Now stop sniveling about my having gotten us a better ship and my having found us a fine healthy young recruit. Let's get down to business. The wind is with us. Let's get on the trail of that French brigantine."

Desmond caught her breath. They would be going after a prize one of these days soon.

She went back to the galley and Bombo. He was finishing scrubbing the pots and hanging them up to gleam in the lantern light. He turned as she came in.

"You found it?"

She nodded and patted the side of the cutlass.

"And now you'll be wanting a hammock. I got you one. It's over there in the corner. You find a spot."

She picked up the hammock.

"Good night, Bombo."

"Good night, boy."

She went out on deck, carrying the hammock.

She could hear voices from below; the men would be down there in the hold. She must find a private spot. She found it under the companionway, just enough room to swing her hammock.

After she had climbed in and curled up she could feel the ship moving slowly. There was a steady breeze abeam and the sea was quiet. The moon was not out but the stars were, not as bright as sometimes, feathery flickerings swimming like little fish in and out of the gray-black clouds. The ship rolled gently, dipping her bowsprit now and then with a whiff of spray. The sea swished softly against the bows.

Dragon was a strange man. It was even stranger that he should call Ned Barnes his friend. Barnes, she realized now, would probably turn out to be no different from that other quartermaster, Batham, on that other ship. She must prepare herself to be just as afraid of him.

Not afraid! Wary. Careful. She could do anything she wanted, as long as she wasn't caught. She had lived by that code back at the Forresters. If you sneaked into the kitchen when the cook wasn't there you could always find a piece of fruit or a bit of pastry that was yours for the taking—if no one saw you. If someone saw you, there would be a beating. She had learned to take beatings in her stride, proudly, never crying out. Never, even when her mother asked her to say she was sorry, would she do so if she wasn't. To Desmond, to lie was a crime. Her feeling had no basis in morality, she was simply acutely aware of herself. Herself was the most important thing in the world. Nothing else mattered.

The Forresters had never called her by name, never tried to make friends. They had referred to her as the brat. Their closest act of recognition was the amusement with which they had watched her play with their boys, when she was a child.

Once she heard Mrs. Forrester say to her mother, "When we took you on, Maria, we did not expect the brat as part of the bargain." Her mother had said, "Nor did I, m'lady," so meekly. Later Desmond understood. During all her growing up she had felt like that—the bad part of a bargain.

That was over now. She was her own self, she was free.

Free, but not happy. Still angry, with the whole world, just for being the way it was.

Barnes was right when he said, a man has to fight, in order to live.

So did a woman.

The ship was quiet.

At last, hand on cutlass, Desmond slept.

For several days, although life was boring, she was not bothered or molested in any way. She learned the names of many of the crew, but she avoided talking to them, or trying to make friends with anyone but old Bombo and a smiling young man named Romley.

Her first assignment was to help Bombo in the galley, and after that she was kept busy polishing brass, swabbing decks, opening the scuppers, and running errands. Nobody paid much attention to her. She only caught glimpses of Dragon and Ned Barnes, who spent their time on the upper deck. Once she felt sure Dragon had left the ship because Barnes was much louder in his commands and demands.

Then, just after dawn one morning, she was awakened by the sound of gunfire and footsteps on the deck.

She guessed immediately what it was.

Timing was important. Between dusk and dawn the prevailing winds blew toward the Atlantic instead of away from it, and that was the time when ships could slip through the islands where the pirates lay in wait. Just before dusk and just after dawn was the prime time for pirates to strike.

She jumped out of her hammock and looked about. The deck was almost deserted. She could see the big French brigantine. The gunfire she had heard was the cannonade that had shattered the brigantine's main mast. The *Poin-*

ciana's small boats were zooming across the water.

One small boat had not been lowered yet. Desmond ran as quickly as she could, hid behind it until she was sure no one was in sight, then climbed inside and covered herself with a tarpaulin.

She would be part of the attack! She would!

As they came closer to the French ship Desmond peeked out from under the tarpaulin. She could see the ship's flag and its name. *Le Carousel*, and hear the noise of the fighting.

She was the last to leave the small boat and climb up the rope ladder they had slung over the side of the ship.

The fighting was far down the deck, and in the interior, the clash of swords and the hallooing were noisy.

Directly in front of her a man lay on the deck. Wounded? Dead?

Neither. He was climbing to his feet, a pistol in his hand.

He raised the gun and fired, but Desmond ducked. Then she ran for the nearest piece of rigging, praying he would not shoot again. As she started to climb she turned her head and saw the gun raised once more. As if her prayer had been answered, the gun did not go off. His arm dropped as a bullet struck him and he fell on his back with a horrible groan, and then lay still.

Now some of the others were emerging from

the cabin, their swords clashing as they moved. It was difficult in the early morning light to distinguish the pirates from the ship's defenders.

She was ready to help with the fight. But where? How?

She moved a bit farther up the rigging for a better look.

Now she could see a dashing French officer with his brocaded jacket and his plumed hat, his neatly trimmed beard. His slender face was all surprise, but he plunged his sword forward with swift sure thrusts, over and over again, outmaneuvering one of the pirates. Some of the other Frenchmen were not doing so well. Several were lying on the deck, moaning. As it grew lighter the streaks of blood flowing over the wood became clear.

Intermittently pistols were fired, usually only inflicting wounds, and as a wounded man staggered back a cutlass would slash across him.

I must attack, Desmond kept thinking. *I must climb down from here and help one of our men.*

Suddenly she spotted Dragon. He had moved to the edge of the deck, not far below her, and was looking down toward the small boats. He called down, "Romley! Bardwell! Rope!"

Within a moment a coil of rope landed on the deck beside him. Again he called out, this time to one of the men near the cabin door.

"Tie up the ones inside, then these."

So the fighting was almost over and she had had no part of it. She had clung there to the rigging, doing nothing.

Now and then a cutlass swung, a knife slashed out, but little by little the scene was quieting. Several men were busy with ropes with those who had not been wounded, or only wounded slightly. The tide had turned, but had the battle been won?

For now she again noticed the Frenchman with the brocaded jacket. He had left the fight, had stepped adroitly behind the mainmast.

She watched him moving slowly and carefully from his hiding place, moving toward Dragon's back, his sword extended.

Desmond took hold of her cutlass.

With a yell, she jumped.

7.

At first Lilias could only stare in disbelief at Roderick Gresham, standing outside of her door in the middle of the night. It could not be possible. She must be dreaming.

Very quietly, as if it were not unusual, he asked, "May I come in?"

Still stunned, and not yet fully awake, she stepped back and allowed him to walk through the doorway.

She still could only stare as he closed the door behind him and bolted it, and stood smiling at her in the candlelight.

"You should not open your door to anyone who tries the lock," he told her.

"I thought . . . it was Ian."

"But it wasn't. It could have been anyone. You are lucky that it was me."

She knew she was shaking; she could find no answer; she turned her head in embarrassment.

"There is no need for you to look so frightened." He took off his hat and put it on the little table. The plume wrapped itself around the candlestick. His black hair, long and curly, brushed the shoulders of his broadcloth jacket, contrasted with the white ruffles of his shirt front.

"Why . . . why did you come, Mr. Gresham?" she managed to ask.

"You may call me Roderick, Lilias. Don't look surprised. Of course I know your name. I know a lot about you. That you are lonely, that you are bored." He looked down at her, his black eyes sweeping over her body. "You are more beautiful than before. No bonnet to hide the silk of your hair, no hoops to hide your slenderness. Soft. You are so soft, Lilias."

"Mr. Gresham . . . Roderick . . ." She was stammering. "Why . . . why did you come?" she repeated.

His eyes never left her face.

"Don't you know?"

He took a step toward her, his large body between her and the candlelight. He reached down his long arms and swept her off her feet, held her close against him so tightly that breathing was a pain.

When he set her down again she backed a step away from him.

"Roderick, please! Please don't!"

"Lilias, don't be afraid of me. I shall not hurt you."

She told herself she must turn and run, but she could not move.

He ran his big hand across her hair, he bent and caressed her ears, her eyelids, her throat with his lips, then his lips reached hers and held them as his arms had held her body. There was no escape.

She wanted nothing now but this complete physical possession. It was as if her life, up to this moment, had been one long trail through a lonely night, and now she had come home, at last.

She threw her arms around his neck and pressed herself against him. He kissed her again and again, as if he would never stop, and when at last he did he ran his hands down her body; it was as she had dreamed only a few hours before.

He unbuttoned the top of her nightdress and put his hand inside and cupped one breast.

"The bed, my darling." It was a breathless whisper. "Where is the bed?"

With his arm around her, his hand still caressing her breast, she led him through the dark across the room and through the bedroom door. She was like one possessed, her whole body alive with the fire of her wanting.

Starlight, through the shutters, only faintly illuminated the white of the sheets.

Again he picked her up, then put her down upon the bed and slowly opened the rest of the buttons on her nightdress. He sat on the side of the bed and bent and kissed one breast and then the other until they were firm and upright and she cried out in ecstasy. Then, abruptly, he pulled away the long sleeves of her gown, jerked the garment from her body and tossed it aside.

She could hear his heavy breathing, and her own; the sounds were loud in the night. She closed her eyes and let the feeling of fire creep over her naked body.

He moved away and she felt her whole self quivering. She gave a little moan, and whispered, "Hurry! Hurry!"

At last he was back, his naked body lying close beside her. He kissed her mouth, her breasts, he parted her legs and kissed her there, and then he was on top of her and entering her and her body was bathed in ecstasy and completion and triumph, and nothing, nothing else in the whole world would ever matter again . . .

At last he fell asleep beside her, his body still pressed close against hers. She was exhausted, but superbly content. The world was a wonderful warm place to be. She had no conscious thought about anything. The world was physical and beautiful, and it was easy to sleep, quickly, like a contented animal.

There was a touch of light in the sky but that was not what had awakened her. It was the slow realization that she was alone in the bed, that he had left her.

She opened her eyes wider and saw him now, beside the bed, pulling his trousers over his legs.

His chest was bare; she could see the curls of black hair, she could remember when they were pressed close against her; she sighed, remembering.

"Roderick . . ." She pronounced his name almost reverently, as if she were saying, "I love you."

He turned and looked down at her, frowning.

"Yes?"

"Roderick!" This time it was as if she were saying, *come back, come back to me*.

"It's almost morning. I must hurry."

"Roderick . . ." This time she found the courage. She sat up in bed. "Roderick, I love you!"

He said, "Yes," again, but this time with a faint smile.

She watched him reach for his ruffled shirt, push his arms into the sleeves, and slowly button it.

"Roderick, don't leave me!"

"I said it was almost morning."

The tone was flat, daytime practical. Abruptly she was conscious of her naked breasts, of her whole body. She grabbed the sheet and pulled it up in front of her.

She watched him smooth at his long black curly hair. He was not looking at her; he did not seem even to be thinking about her. He could have been a stranger. And only a short while ago he had lain next to her, and they had . . .

She felt close to tears as she watched him put

on his jacket. He did not look at her again until he had finished. Then he came back to the bedside, and sat down on the edge of the bed.

She threw her arms around his neck. He held her only for a moment, then he took her arms from his neck and pushed her back down onto the bed.

He put one hand over a breast and held it, so firmly she was afraid there would be a bruise.

He said, "There'll be other times, Lilias. I haven't had my fill of you."

Then he got up from the bed and strode out of the room, so swiftly that her cry of "Roderick!" was echoing in the emptiness.

She cried after he had left, crying because he *had* left, and because the slow realization of what she had done swept over her. She was a married woman and she had behaved like a whore; she had committed an unforgivable sin, from which she could not be absolved by any imaginable confession. How could a sin have been so wonderful? She was ashamed, she was miserable, and yet at the same time every bit of her body was aching for his touch.

She could not let it happen again, and yet, how could she go on living if it did not happen?

He had not spoken of love. Yet he had said, there'll be other times. But there must not be; she must not let that happen!

When it was finally morning, when the birds were caroling away, when she could hear Zula in the kitchen, she realized she could not just lie there, thinking and feeling and regretting, yet remembering.

She climbed out of bed, looked back at the crumpled stained sheets, hurriedly gathered them into a bundle. She must find an excuse to put them to soak before Zula caught sight of them. She hung her nightdress in the commode, took down the robe she had not used last night, wrapped it around her, opened the door to the bedroom, and called out to Zula to fill a tub for a bath.

The tub was brought to the bedroom and Zula, as she went in and out bringing pitchers of water, looked somewhat curious at this unusual time for a request for a bath.

Never had Lilias scrubbed so vigorously. But she could not wash the feeling from her lips, nor indeed from any part of her.

She dried and dressed slowly, dumped the sheets and her nightgown into the tub, and pushed them about. She was just finishing when Zula knocked on her door.

She called out, "Come in!" Zula did, and immediately looked at the tub with the laundry floating in it.

"Madame is not well?"

"No, I'm not. I'm afraid I ate and drank too much at the reception, and have thrown up. I shan't want breakfast."

"I'm sorry, Ma'am."

"I'll be all right." She avoided Zula's eyes. "I'll just rest this morning."

"I'll put clean sheets on the bed."

"Thank you."

She sat by the window while Zula removed the tub, came back with clean linens, and re-made the bed. She watched the woman lacka-daisically, as if it were a scene in a play, as if the whole process had nothing to do with her. And when Zula had left she lay down on top of the bedspread, watching the golden morning sun slant through the shutters.

This was her real world; this was her life. After awhile she would have to get up and go about her usual routines: a bit of mending, a bit of reading, a bit of flower picking and arranging in the pitchers that served as vases.

She must forget what had happened. She must pretend that it never happened.

As the next few days passed, she was lonelier than ever, waiting for Ian's return. She dreaded that return, and paradoxically longed for it.

Ian was seldom off island on a Sunday, but this time he was. There was no church service, no reason to dress up or to have a big dinner. She gave Zula the afternoon off to go see her relatives on the other side of the island.

About two o'clock the sky abruptly darkened, lightning flashed, the thunder boomed and the rain came down in torrents. Lilias, who was terrified by thunder, hurried to close the shutters.

Then she lit a candle and tried to read, to lose herself in some familiar old story so that she would be able to ignore the thunder. It was no use. Each time the thunder roared she dropped the book and held her hands over her ears.

Then, as she lowered her hands, she heard another sound that made her jump to her feet.

Someone was pounding on the front door.

Could it be Roderick again? In broad daylight?

She half opened the shutter on the window by the front door and peeked out.

Jonathan's carriage and donkey were in the driveway.

She hurried to open the door.

"Jonathan, come in! Come in!"

He did not hesitate. He stood on the doormat, shaking water from his jacket, taking off his hat to shake it.

"I feel like a drowned rat."

"You look like one." Of course he didn't. His back was straight as ever, his sharp blue eyes were twinkling.

"Thank you very much. Your flattery should be returned somehow. You look like . . ."

"What do I look like?"

"You don't look like the parson's wife. Where's your Sunday dress?"

"There was no service today."

"I know. That's why I took the liberty of coming to call."

"That's sweet of you, Jonathan."

She felt suddenly a little shy. She said quickly, "What are we doing standing here? Come in and take off your jacket while I get you some tea. Before you catch your death of cold."

She was already in the kitchen before she remembered that Zula was not there. The kitchen was empty; her cold supper laid out on the table under a cover; the fire was out.

Jonathan got up from his chair as she came back into the living room.

"I'm sorry, I forgot. I gave Zula the afternoon off. The fire's out. Oh, Jonathan, I'm so sorry!"

"So Zula isn't here. That makes it a bit awkward, doesn't it?"

One simply didn't call on a married woman unless there were some sort of chaperone. Jonathan felt somewhat uncomfortable.

"No, it's not awkward." But there was no real assurance in her voice. "It's just that I can't give you tea."

"That's quite all right," he said quickly. "But, all the same, I think I should leave."

He did not want to leave. He had been unable to get Lilias out of his mind ever since the night he accompanied her to the reception.

"Not until the rain stops," she was saying. "You'd only get drenched again. Now take off your jacket and hang it on that chair to dry."

He obeyed.

They were still standing when the lightning flashed again, and when the thunder roared

105

Lilias instinctively moved closer to Jonathan. She put her hands over her ears and stood there trembling.

Jonathan patted her shoulder with a shaky hand.

As the thunder faded and the rain began to roar she took her hands from her ears and cried out, "Oh, Jonathan, I'm so glad you came! I'm so afraid of thunder!"

"I can't do much about the thunder," he said wrily.

"But you're here!" she said shakily. "That's all that matters!"

She threw her arms around his neck and pressed close against him.

She could feel his heart beating very rapidly, as hers was. The thunder had stopped. The rain was pounding down on the roof with a steady, rhythmic beat, like their hearts.

She turned her head and looked straight into his face, into those piercing blue eyes.

Except for the small circle of candlelight, the shuttered room was dark as night. He had thought of this so many times, he had imagined what it would be like to be alone with Lilias, but he had shoved such thoughts aside. Ian was his friend, he must not covet Ian's wife. But here they were. And the way she was clinging to him! The thunder was only an excuse, he felt sure.

Her face was close to his, her lips parted. It seemed the most natural thing in the world to kiss her. Her lips were sweet and soft but they clung to his as her body was clinging.

When at last the kiss was finished, she was limp against him. He put his hands on her slender shoulders and then let his hands slide down her back, very gently, until they reached the curve of her buttocks. To touch her, just to touch her!

There were plenty of women to be had on Cabra—black and white and in-between—but never had he found one like this, delicate but filled with passion.

He took her arms from around his neck and pulled her down on the settee beside him. He held both her hands, and kissed the palms.

"So you are afraid of thunder."

"Yes!"

"There is something you should be more afraid of, dear Lilias."

"What is that?"

"Yourself, Lilias."

"What do you mean?" Genuinely confused, she nevertheless felt a sharp twinge of apprehension.

He was holding her hands, so tightly that she could not break away.

"Because of what happened, just now, between us."

"But it just *happened*, Jonathan. We couldn't help it."

She had felt so safe, so content, in his arms. It had been a moment out of context with any part of her life, a moment of sheer comfort and joy.

"But we mustn't let it happen again. I might not be able to control myself. And as for you . . . oh, Lilias you are so ready, so very ready."

"Ready?" She knew exactly what he meant but somehow she wanted to hear him say it.

"I have been watching you for a long time," he told her. "You are lonely and unhappy. No, don't shake your head. I'm telling you the truth. There is something about your marriage that isn't right. There is something I could give you. So easily."

She pulled her hands away from his. *I have already been given that something*, she thought, *only the other night. I was given a night of ecstasy; a lifetime of guilt.*

She moved away from him and got to her feet. The rain had stopped as suddenly as it had begun; the sun was out, slanting through the shutters' cracks. Daylight. Reality.

"Jonathan, you must not speak of such things ever again. Never!" Her guilt made her angry.

"Never?" He smiled at her anger, as strong as her response to his touch. *I wouldn't lay a wager on that*, he thought. *This woman is ripe for the picking.*

She had turned her head. Over her shoulder she said in a small voice, "Jonathan, would you please leave?"

"As you wish."

Still not facing him, she added, "We'll just forget about this afternoon."

"Will we?" He got to his feet, walked past her to the entryway and picked up his hat and jacket.

"Good afternoon, Lilias."

He slammed the door behind him.

Ian came home as usual, tired, grubby, taciturn, one afternoon. He said little before he had bathed and rested: again as usual.

She asked Zula to cook the joint of mutton they had saved for some special occasion. She tiptoed about, dressing in not a special dress, but one that Ian once had admired—and since Ian seldom seemed aware of any of her clothes, that made this one special. She brushed her hair until it was sleek, she peered into her little mirror wondering if her guilt would show in her eyes.

She wondered again when he later emerged from the bedroom and stood looking at her for a moment. She was sitting in a chair near the candlelit dining table with her embroidery. The needle work helped to steady her hands as she looked up at him.

Why wasn't it you, Ian? she thought. *Oh, why wasn't it you!*

Ian looked at the silver candlesticks, at the red hibiscus blossoms she had arranged in a silver bowl.

"Are we expecting guests?"

"No, it's just welcome home."

"It's beautiful. And so are you." He spoke shyly. She looked down at her embroidery.

"I don't tell you that often enough, do I?" Ian went on. He came over beside her and put his hand on her shoulder. "Perhaps it's because I've been away, but somehow tonight you seem particularly beautiful. Somehow . . . radiant."

As if embarrassed by his own words, he walked over to the window and looked out into the late afternoon.

Her face was growing warm. She was relieved, and when he spoke again, he was still staring out at the sunset.

"Lilias, my dear, could it possibly be that you are . . . that we . . ."

Dear God, he thinks I am with child!

"Oh, no. No, Ian, I'm sure." She put down her needle work; her hands were shaking too hard to go on with that pretense at busyness.

He turned and came back to her, and again put his hand on her shoulder.

"It's all right, my dear. Really. You must not be upset by my asking."

She *was* upset, but not by his asking; by the sudden realization of the possible consequences of that night with Roderick. She must pray each night that the monthly sickness would come. Her shame was punishment enough.

Ian took her hands in his and pulled her to

her feet, so that they were facing each other directly.

"You must not mind," he said. "You must not think that I am disappointed. Everything will come, in good time, and in the meanwhile I am happy. You are everything a wife could be to me, and more."

She burst into tears. He put his arms around her and held her close. He patted her shoulder, murmuring, "There, there!" She wanted to cry out to him, *Ian, you don't know what I am, what I've done,* but she could not do it, she dared not do it, for she would be lost without Ian's love and protection.

When she had finished crying and wiped her eyes, she hurried into the bedroom to the washbowl and washed her face.

She returned to the dining room, and Ian smiled. "Better now?"

She nodded.

"Good."

At the dinner table he said, "Doctor Manning told me something today."

Doctor? Oh, please, don't get back on the subject of babies! She did her best to keep her expression calm. "Oh?"

"There is now a dressmaker in Edwardsville. A Madame Collette."

She tried not to show her relief too obviously.

"I thought you might like to pay her a visit. Perhaps get a new frock or two. Lilias, what's the matter? I thought you'd be pleased."

111

"Ian, I am!" Pleased, relieved, and surprised. "But can we afford it?"

A shadow crossed his face.

"Of course we can afford it," he said shortly.

The dressmaker, Madame Collette, was an escaped slave from Martinique. She had been the dressmaker for a wealthy French planter's family, lived in their house, and was somewhat of an aristocrat in her own right. She was tall and slender; her color was *cafe au lait*, and her accent West Indian with the lilt of French.

"The choice of yard goods on this island is deplorable, *deplorable*, but we shall make do; we shall do what we can do with what is available. I promise you style, whatever shabby goods you are able to find. Come, let us measure you!"

She went about measurng in a truly professional style, then told Lilias the amount of material needed for a gown, and sent her next door to the draper's.

Lilias was sitting on a stool at the counter, deciding between a somber linsey-woolsey and a bright silk organza, when a voice she could recognize all too easily said merely, "Good afternoon," in a tone just a notch above a whisper.

She replied, "Good afternoon," in an equally quiet voice before she dared to look at him.

It was strange how just the sight of this man, just the sound of his voice, could dissolve her.

Her breasts were growing tight underneath her bodice; her breath was growing short.

The saleslady stepped into the back room for another bolt of goods.

In an even lower voice Roderick asked, "When can I see you again?"

Lilias shook her head. "No. *No*."

"When is he going away again? When can I come again?" It was as if he did not even hear her protest.

Lilias shook her head once more. "You must not."

"Then when can we meet?"

"We must not meet."

He touched her arm. "We shall."

She looked up at him, pleading.

He was smiling. "Your husband need never know." His eyes were twinkling. "Unless I tell him."

8.

Desmond's scream as she jumped from the rigging, cutlass in hand, turned every face upward.

She landed squarely on the Frenchman's back and knocked him flat upon the deck; his sword fell from his hand. Now was the time to show them what she could do, to prove herself. She lifted her cutlass high above the man's back.

"Hold that." Dragon's voice.

She looked up at him, all surprise. Here she had been ready to stretch her courage to the breaking point and actually slash the man's neck. The cutlass shook in her hand.

"Get off this ship! This is an order!"

As she got to her feet she saw Dragon picking up the Frenchman's sword, and heard him say, "Tie him up." Then he turned to her. "Go back where you belong. Who gave you permission to come aboard here?"

"Nobody." How could he look so angry? She had jumped to save his life. She *had* saved his life. He should be grateful; he should have told her to go ahead and cut the man's throat.

114

Again she lifted the cutlass, furious with him, determined to show her mettle. But Dragon's arm shot out and he took the weapon from her, tucked it into his own belt. He just stood looking at her with clear, cold gray eyes, relentless as the dragon for which he was named.

She moved between the fallen wounded to the side of the ship. In a way she was relieved to be banished, but she still was resentful.

Some of the boats were starting back. She climbed down the ladder and dropped into the second in line. She sat down beside the man named Romley, who turned and grinned at her.

"Good work, boy!" He slapped her on the back.

The praise was gratifying; it was what she had wanted, had expected.

As she climbed aboard the *Poinciana* she could hear a small "Huzzah!" She looked up. The men who had come back on the boat ahead of her were all looking down at her, smiling.

She was one of them, now.

She looked up at the fading stars. The other boats and men would soon be coming back on board with the ship's treasures, whatever they were; soon they would sail away, leaving the Frenchmen to get free of the ropes, to mend their wounds, to set sail again for wherever they were headed, without their cargo.

She climbed to the poop deck to stand beside old Bombo, who had been left in charge, and watched the men come back, to pile up bags and chests on the main deck. Ned and Dragon came aboard last of all, walked past her without looking at her, and went in the great cabin.

"You rascal!"

She turned. Bombo was grinning at her.

"You're in for a bit of trouble, lad. Stealing a cutlass. Boarding without an order."

"But I proved myself! I showed what I could do!"

"You did that."

There was the sound of the anchor being pulled up, the sails began to draw, the *Poinciana* was moving.

Suddenly Ned Barnes was standing beside them.

He looked from one to the other, as if he were a little surprised to see them together. Then he smiled sarcastically.

"Time for bed for both of you."

"Yes, sir," Bombo agreed.

Barnes turned to Desmond.

"You," he said. "I want you to stay out of my sight, until I want you. Until I send for you. Do you understand?"

"Yes, sir." But she lifted her chin.

He frowned at that.

"Where did you get that cutlass?"

"I found it."

"Where?"

"In the bosun's hold."

Barnes whirled to old Bombo.

116

"You told him?" he guessed.

Desmond cried out, "No, I found it myself!" She didn't want to get old Bombo in trouble.

"I told him, sir," Bombo said quietly. "I thought it would do no harm," he added meekly.

"No harm!"

"I had no idea the lad would show his mettle, the way he did."

For a moment the quartermaster stared angrily at the old man. Then he said, "Come along, Bombo, I want to talk to you. Without the brat." He gave a jerk of his head and walked away and Bombo followed.

Brat. Desmond seethed. Then she reminded herself: *you've got to keep your temper, you've got to!* But right now she was too tired even to be angry. She went back to her hammock, curled up, and this time was able to sleep.

She woke to broad daylight, a gray daylight because of a lowering sky. She could smell food. It had been a long time since the last meal.

First she went beyond the galley to the pantry in search of the water-breaker, so that she could wash. It was not hard to find, but the tub of water already was smelling a bit foul. She dipped in her hands and brushed lightly at her face. Instead of going directly back to the galley she moved forward, to a part of the ship she

117

had not explored before, trusting she would find another exit to the quarter deck.

Just as light outlined a doorway in front of her she heard a small noise, a groan. She turned her head, saw Bombo in a corner, in irons, and ran to him.

"Oh, Bombo, why? Why did they do this to you?"

"Barnes had several reasons," he said weakly.

"Your telling me where the cutlasses were?"

"That was only one."

"What else, Bombo?" She squatted beside him.

"I fell asleep on watch. Twice."

"But he shouldn't put you in chains for that. Me and my cutlass must have been what did it."

"The last straw, mebbe," he agreed.

"How long do you have to be like this?"

"Twenty-four hours, he says. I don't mind, too much. These chains are uncomfortable and a nuisance but it's better than twenty-four lashes of that cat-o-nine-tails. Don't worry about me, boy, I've been through this before. The worst that can happen is that I'll get hungry." He gave a wry laugh. "So may the rest of you, without a real cook."

"No! And you won't get hungry. I'll go get you something right now."

"Don't you do that, lad! It'll only get you in trouble," he protested.

"Don't you worry about me!" Desmond

cried. "You're my friend and I'm not going to let you go hungry!"

He called after her as she ran through the door into the daylight. "No, lad, no!" but she paid no attention.

Back on deck she found they were dishing out some sort of fish chowder into coconut shells, chowder that Bombo must have made before he was put in chains. She noticed that some were coming back for second helpings, so it would be easy to take her first helping down to Bombo.

Bombo shook his head in disapproval but he accepted the bowl of chowder and soon was happily dipping out pieces of fish with his fingers and chewing away.

After a few bites he asked, "Why you being so good to me, boy? What's your name again?"

"Desmond. I like you; you're my friend. I don't want you to go hungry." She was thinking that having a friend was nice, and of how few she had had. There was Obie, of course. Older men were her friends. Maybe they were like fathers, and she'd never had a real father. Oh, maybe she had a father, somewhere, but he didn't even know she existed. French. Like that man on the ship she had been ready to kill. Had her father been like that? Handsome and graceful?

You're thinking about men, Desmond, and you'd thought you hated them. You're thinking like a woman, and you shouldn't be.

119

Bombo tipped the coconut shell and drank. Then he asked, "Why did you run away from home, Desmond? or did you run away? Were you captured, the way I was?"

Why had she run away from home? She didn't want to tell him that story. She said, carefully, "This time I was captured. There wasn't a fight or anything like that, but the quartermaster just decided to take me along. What could I do?"

"You didn't answer my first question."

"No."

"You don't want to talk about yourself."

"No."

"So be it." He handed her the empty coconut shell. "Hurry. Get some for yourself."

"No!" The shell was knocked from Bombo's hand. Bombo and Desmond looked up into Ned Barnes' angry face.

"What's the meaning of this?" the quartermaster demanded.

"The lad meant no harm," Bombo said gently.

For an answer Barnes slapped Desmond across the face. "Go to the poop deck! Now!"

Desmond, her face stinging from the slap, turned away toward the light in the doorway. Barnes was at her heels. He struck her again from behind, then pushed her along the deck. Every time she faltered or hesitated, he struck her, and in the end was dragging her.

Desmond made no sound. She was thoroughly afraid now, most of all afraid that he would discover she was a girl, and there would be that battle to fight again, and this time she might not be so lucky.

It was starting to rain. The ship rocked a little, and her bare feet skidded on the slippery deck. She would have cried out for help, but that might give away her secret. And who would come? Who would care? Only old Bombo, and he was in chains.

At last they reached the ladder to the poop deck and climbed up.

"I've had enough of your insolence."

She watched him reach for the whip. She gritted her teeth and took a deep breath.

It was much harsher than the whippings she had received back on Barbados from the Forresters and from her mother. But she tried to pretend it was just the same thing, and as usual her pride kept her from screaming out. The punishment was unjust. To feed a hungry old man was not a crime, and even taking the cutlass and joining the fight was not a crime. She was good and Barnes was evil, and when you could not fight evil agressively there was nothing to do but to submit, with your body, but not your soul, and her sharp eyes, whenever she faced him, were eloquent with defiance.

It seemed forever before he stopped, and just as he did Dragon came out on deck.

"What are you doing, Ned?" His voice was quiet, but icy.

"Can't you see?" Ned grated hoarsely.

"Of course I can see. But why?"

"He got out of hand."

"How?"

Barnes flung the whip aside.

"First he stole that cutlass and went aboard the brigantine."

"I know. But he saved my life."

Desmond, rubbing her sore shoulders, looked up in surprise and gratitude.

"But then I found him bringing food to Bombo."

"What about that?" Dragon asked.

"Bombo is in chains."

"Again, why?"

"Someone must maintain discipline on this ship."

Ned's scarred face was flushed with anger as he tried to defend himself.

"Someone is taking liberties himself," Dragon said coldly. "Tell me what old Bombo did."

"Fell asleep on watch. Twice."

"You work him too hard. He's a tailor, remember? Let him be a tailor and a cook."

"He also told the boy where to find a cutlass."

Dragon looked at Desmond.

She said, "He meant no harm. He is a good man."

Dragon went on studying her face, almost as if he were seeing it for the first time. Finally he said, "And so, with that cutlass you came aboard that ship and saved my life."

Desmond was embarrassed now. She was pleased with the captain's expression, quite sure her punishment was over, but awkward at becoming the center of attention, wondering if now he would start asking questions, as Bombo had.

Dragon turned to Barnes.

"For that," he asked, "for saving my life, you were giving him a lashing?"

"I said I caught him taking food to Bombo."

Dragon shook his head and sighed.

"The boy's new," he said to Barnes. "He does not know all your rules. I want you to go this moment and set Bombo free."

Scowling, Barnes tossed back his head, opened his mouth as if he were going to speak but closed it again and strode away.

Again Dragon looked at her with that curious, contemplative expression. So Desmond asked, "Please, sir, may I go have my dinner now?"

"I'm afraid you're too late for that." He hesitated. Then he put his hand on her aching shoulder and said, "Come with me."

He led her into his cabin.

The great cabin seemed the most beautiful room she ever had seen, even grander than the parlor in the Forresters' house, although of course smaller. It had been the captain's quarters when the *Poinciana* had been a Spanish ship. It was paneled in mahogany, the bulk-heads beaded with gilt, with a crimson carpet on the floor. Mahogany chests with brass trim shone in the light of the hanging brass lanterns. On a table was a tray of food . . . roast chicken, slices of meat, jellies, pastries, a de-canter of twinkling red wine.

"Part of our booty," Dragon said. "More than Ned and I could eat. Help yourself. The French at least know how to cook."

She sat down on a straight chair in front of the table. Dragon sat down on a large armchair in a corner. At first she could only stare at the array of food. It was the most lavish banquet she had seen in a long time, not since Christmas back on the Forrester plantation, when she had peeked into the dining room. She felt now as if she were gazing upon forbidden territory, as if he could not mean what he had said.

She looked across at Dragon. He was smiling, as if he understood her disbelief. She was aware of her dirty shirt and trousers, her uncombed hair, her half-washed face. Dragon's clothes were equally rough, but somehow that did not make it right for her to be so untidy. Sitting here in front of the captain she began remem-bering that she was a girl.

"Go ahead," he said. "Try a piece of chicken. It is very good. And I am not partial to fowl."

She picked up a chicken leg and took a bite. It was good. She took another bite, and then another, chewing and swallowing rapidly, as if

124

the food were a mirage and would disappear if she did not hurry. Hunger had dissolved her awkwardness.

Dragon sat there in silence while she ate, only getting up once to pour her a glass of the red wine. It was a beautiful crystal clear goblet, and her fingers carefully around the stem and held it daintily, as she had seen the mistress do long ago.

"Where do you come from, Desmond?"

"Barbados," she said, reaching now for the pastry.

"But you have a French name."

"My father was French."

"And a gentleman."

She put down the bit of pastry she had been eating and looked at Dragon. "I don't know," she told him. "I never knew my father. Why do you say he was a gentleman?"

"I am guessing that you were gently born."

"What makes you say that?"

"I'm not sure. The way you speak. Your table manners. You're a rather unusual boy. And so, as I said, I'm guessing you were gently born and for some reason ran away from home and went to sea."

When Bombo had said, you don't want to talk about yourself, she had agreed. But somehow Dragon made her want to talk, to tell him at least some of her story.

"I did run away," she said. "And, like you said, I'm unusual. But not the way you think."

"Oh?"

She finished eating the little pastry, while deciding exactly what to tell him, and exactly how.

"I'm a bastard," she said at last. "And so was my mother. And she is a slave, a white slave. And there was no place for me in the house where I grew up, and so I ran away."

"And decided to become a pirate. Or wasn't that your choice?"

"If being a pirate will make me rich, that's what I want to be."

"It's a rough life."

"But it's a decent one! That's what . . . what I heard him—the quartermaster—say to you."

Dragon gave a little laugh, as if he were amused by what he must suspect was eavesdropping. He got up and poured himself a glass of the red wine, and sipped it.

"That's Ned's opinion," he said at last. "Not mine."

"But you're friends," she protested.

"Yes, we've been friends for a long while. Almost all my life. I owe a lot to Ned. You see, when I was only a little toddler, he saved my life. I owe my life to him. As I owe it today, to you." He looked down into his wine glass. "Ned was a brave boy, and he's a brave man. And even though there are many, many things about which we disagree, he is my friend."

The way he said the *friend* told her a lot,

told her why he had understood how she felt about Bombo.

"So being rich is important to you," Dragon said thoughtfully, looking down into his wine glass again.

"Yes, it is!"

"Were you so very poor? Were you starving as so many people are in this world?"

"No, not really. But we were no more than slaves, my mother and I. We lived in a house that belonged to rich people and I could see them having things and doing things that I couldn't."

"I see. What would being rich mean to you?"

"It would mean having beautiful clothes and . . ." She almost said jewels, but hastily added ". . . and having food like this and dishes and glasses like these every day. And a beautiful big home, and servants."

And a husband, she thought to herself. A quiet, gentle man, like this one.

Suddenly the ship swerved. The wine bottle started to slide down the table. Dragon grabbed it and put it up on a little shelf with a protective railing around the rim.

Then he asked, "Have you had enough to eat?"

"Oh, yes. Yes, thank you, sir."

He was dismissing her. She had stayed much too long, of course. She had enjoyed the food, and his company, so much that she almost had forgotten where she was and who she was.

Dragon said, "I must go out on deck and see what this is all about. I'm afraid we're off course. You better run along, boy, they might need you to climb the rigging. You're the nearest thing to a monkey we've got aboard."

"Thank you for the food."

"All right. It's all right, this time, but we mustn't make it a habit. Bad for morale." He smiled.

She wished her hair was not cut off, but long and piled high atop her head, that she was wearing a beautiful dress all full of ruffles; she wished she were a girl again and that he knew she was a girl. She wished a thousand things as he put his hand on her shoulder and again said, "Run along, boy."

A storm had broken by the time she reached the main deck. The wind and rain were slashing across the ship, the sails had been furled and the *Poinciana* rocked back and forth like a helpless piece of driftwood. Water was pouring in the scupper holes. No need to climb the rigging for any purpose; all she could do was to huddle out of the rain along with the others.

On the horizon was a blob of land barely visible through the rain.

"Oh, God, Pollino!" the man called Freedman cried. "We can't put in there. Foxy, look!"

"We may have to." Foxy told the bosun.

"What's Pollino?" Desmond asked. Nobody asnwered her. She made her way along the deck to where Romly stood hanging onto a capstan, and looking toward the land.

"What's Pollino?" she asked again.

"Don't you know? It's an Indian island. Nothing but those deadly Caribs on this side. Savages. Dirty savages." Romley spit over the railing.

Desmond thought: my grandmother was a Carib. Mother talked about her as a person, as a human being, not a dirty savage, even though that same woman sold my mother into slavery.

Maria had said, "My mother was a chief's daughter and proud of it. She acted like a princess, always, although all she wore was that short apron of a skirt, strung with beads. You must never be ashamed of your Indian blood."

She had held out her hands in a strange way, the way she did each night when she tucked Desmond in bed. It was a kind of blessing that only her mother gave, something that she must have carried away with her when she was sent away from her Indian home and sold to the Forresters.

And yet Romly had called them dirty savages, as if he hated them—and feared them.

9.

The saleslady came back just as Roderick teased Lilias about speaking to Ian.

Roderick touched his plumed hat. "Good day, Mrs. Everett." He turned and strode out of the shop.

The saleslady asked, "Which does madame prefer, the linsey-woolsey, or the organza?"

Lilias stared blankly at the bolts of goods.

"Both," she said. "I'll take both."

"Very well."

Lilias reached for her reticule. It took all the money Ian had given her to pay for the yard goods.

She gathered up the materials after the saleslady had measured and cut, and then dashed next door to Madame Collette's.

The woman's eyes went up as Lilias put the materials on her table.

"Both, madame?"

"Both!" she said firmly.

Madame Collette shrugged, felt the materials.

"This gray, this linsey-woolsey is so drab. However, if we can find some trim . . ." She looked up at Lilias. "Madame, you look distraught," she said finally.

"I'm sorry. What were you saying?"

Madame smiled. "These dresses will have style, Mistress Everett. Be assured. Come back next Wednesday."

"Thank you."

Lilias stood for a moment, trying to compose herself before she went out into the sunshine to meet Ian by Government House.

He was waiting for her under the portico of the building, stepped out quickly and hurried to meet her.

"Lilias, my dear, you're pale! Is something wrong?"

"No." She wished she had thought to pinch some color into he rcheeks.

"You have finished with Madame Collette?"

"Oh, yes."

"And you found the material for the frock?"

"Ian, I'm afraid I bought material for two dresses. I spent all the money you gave me."

"That's quite all right."

"I'm to come back next Wednesday. To the dressmaker's, for my first fitting. She seems like a good dressmaker, not the same as the woman in London where Aunt Rachel always took me, but all the same she seemed intelligent."

She went on talking, rambling about the dressmaker, about the colors she had chosen. She was not sure if what she was saying would interest Ian, but she couldn't bear for there to be silence between them; she didn't want to have to look him in the eye. They walked down the street, side by side, nodding to passersby, to where the cart was waiting.

Before the next appointment with the dressmaker Ian decided to teach her how to drive the donkey cart.

She was excited and a little frightened, but Billy was a docile donkey, and, as Ian pointed out, when he was called away it would be convenient for her to go visiting or into town to shop. Besides, "Next week, you know, I shall be off island again."

Ian must have realized her loneliness and boredom. Perhaps Jonathan had talked to him?

They made several trips to town, Lilias holding the reins and Ian watching. She was surprised to find how much fun it was to guide that little donkey. She talked to Billy along the road. Ian laughed at her, but he looked pleased that she was happy. Driving that donkey did give her a sense of self-confidence.

There came the day when she drove Ian to his sloop on the waterfront and reluctantly watched him leave. Three days? Four? He did not know when he would be back. He only said, "Soon."

She drove home alone to find that a letter had been delivered during her absence.

It was an invitation from Rowena Gresham for Lilias to come to tea.

She did not want to go for tea at the Greshams. But she could think of no excuse, so of course she would have to accept. She dreaded facing the eagle eye of Mrs. Gresham, who might be aware of her husband's proclivities.

She wished that one of her new dresses were finished for this occasion, but they weren't, and she was obliged to wear something she had worn a dozen times before, and, she was sure, in Rowena Gresham's presence. But then she thought that this might be better, might help to allay Rowena's suspicions of that dowdy little mouse, the parson's wife.

The day of the party she brought her hostess a bouquet of bougainvillaea, her favorite bougainvillaea, the color of tea roses. It turned out to be a foolish gesture, as Mrs. Gresham's drawing room was full of flowers from her own garden. Mrs. Gresham received the bouquet with polite disdain, handed it to her maid to put in water. The bougainvillaea did not reappear in the drawing room.

There was no sign of Roderick.

The children were there with their mother. One little boy, one little girl, daintily dressed, big-eyed and shy. The little boy was scrawny, a bit cross-eyed, but the little girl had her father's coloring, and the same curly black hair. Lilias caught her breath. Children. He had fathered two children. Could it happen again, with her? She tried to drive such thoughts from her mind, to smile at the two, as if they were anyone's children, as they politely curtsied.

She was grateful when the black maid came and took them away.

She sat down on one of the stiff chairs; she mentioned that her husband was off island. Mrs. Gresham expressed sympathy for her being alone. Lilias told of driving the donkey and cart but her hostess' reaction was not one of congratulations so much as criticism. She had the opinion that it was not proper for a minister's wife to drive about the countryside alone, in a cart.

Lilias tried talking about the flowers—a safe subject—but Mrs. Gresham waved that subject aside. Her gardener grew them, her maids arranged them. She only enjoyed looking at them and did not know the names of any of them.

Lilias tried a bit of man talk: how the war was progesssing, how much danger there might be from the French. Mrs. Gresham did not know, and cared less. She did say, "My husband's sympathies are not entirely with the British, you understand. After all, his mother was French. Besides, as he tells me, this is the New World. We should have our own country; we should not get involved with those old European quarrels."

There were tiny sandwiches and dainty iced cakes, and excellent true English tea, but Lilias had no appetite. She kept wondering why she had been invited.

It came out at last, just as she was to take her leave. Mrs. Gresham wished to announce that her husband was going to make a big donation to the church.

"I am sure my husband will be very pleased."

"He should be."

Lilias did not like the way Rowena Gresham said it. It was not just that it put her so definitely in the position of being the poor parson's wife, whose daily bread depended on contributions. There was something else in Rowena's tone, that made her wonder if the woman had guessed what had happened between her husband and Lilias.

Lilias said, "I shall tell him the moment he returns. I'm sure he will want to thank you, in person."

Lilias put down her tea cup and got to her feet. "Thank you so much, Mrs. Gresham, for the lovely tea. But I really must leave now. I've only been driving for a few days and I'd like to get home before dark."

"Of course." Again the big nose was raised in the air, again that smile of contempt. Now it was easy to believe the story of her poisoning the pirates.

Before Lilias could take one step Roderick walked into the room.

"Am I late for tea?"

"No, you are not too late," Rowena said

coldly. "You are just in time to see Mrs. Everett to the door."

Lilias gave a little bow and crossed the room. Roderick stood aside to let her pass and then followed her out into the front hall.

He opened the door for her but as she started through he grabbed her arm. He whispered, "Tomorrow afternoon. This time. The springs."

"The springs?"

"The hot springs. Be there."

She shook her head.

His arms went around her and held her tightly. He crushed his mouth against hers and she went limp in his arms, slowly accepting the kiss and then helplessly responding.

He released her.

"You see how it must be, Lilias," he whispered. Then he stepped back and in his natural rich voice he said, perhaps a bit loudly, "Good afternoon, Mrs. Everett. I am truly sorry I arrived so late."

"Good afternoon, Mr. Gresham."

She stepped outside and he closed the door behind her.

She was completely shaken, by the conversation with Mrs. Gresham, by the whole visit from beginning to end, and by Roderick's whispered words and his kiss. She felt unsteady as she walked down the steps and through the garden, wondering if her hostess were watching from a window, wondering what she might be saying to Roderick.

She climbed into her cart, and looked up at the house. Only Roderick was watching from a window in another part of the house opposite the drawing room. He lifted one hand in farewell.

She told herself over and over again that she would not go to the springs. She would not even consider meeting Roderick.

But all that night she dreamed of him. She tossed and turned in that lonely bed and the physical remembrance was almost overpowering.

By morning light she told herself, *you will not go. You must not go.*

She moved restlessly about the little house; she tried reading but it was no good.

Noon passed. Ian's big old clock bonged out the hours. Teatime. The springs. A good hour's drive.

Her resolve faded.

Your husband need never know. No one need ever know. Besides, he may only want to meet me there to talk to me. To make plans. Daytime makes everything safe and reasonable.

She hurried to get out of her morning dress, to put on a pretty white dress with little clusters of flowers embroidered all over it, a low neckline that would be cool on the long hot ride, a bonnet that tied under her chin with a yellow ribbon. No hoops. It was too warm for hoops.

Thank goodness the servants here were not as nosey as they had been back in Aunt Rachel's house in England. She did not have to say a word to Zula about where she was going, or why.

The springs were on the other side of town, in the same direction as the Greshams' house, so she had to drive through town to get there. Would anyone notice her? The streets were not crowded at that hour. But just as she passed Government House she saw Jonathan coming out the door. She reined the donkey and stopped to say hello.

"You look very happy, madame," was his greeting. "I assume you are happy driving all by yourself."

"Oh, yes!"

"I told Ian you would like to."

"I thought you might have."

Again she felt awkward with Jonathan. She had the uncanny feeling that he might suspect what she was doing.

"This way you are free to go shopping. Or calling on friends, when Ian is away."

"That's right. He's off island now. Besides, it's fun driving Billy. He's a nice donkey, not at all stubborn, like other donkeys."

"Better stick with Billy," he said blandly.

Was that another warning?

"I haven't seen much of you lately, Lilias,"

he added. If you haven't had tea elsewhere, why don't you stop back here at Government House on your way home?"

"Thank you, Jonathan. If it's not too late."

She had never once thought of time. Unconsciously she flipped the reins and Billy began to move. She waved goodby to Jonathan.

She drove more slowly, disturbed by the meeting with Jonathan, more conscious of her deceit, through Edwardsville's one street. Then she was out of town, past the entrance to the Gresham plantation. The road crossed Cabra's one tiny river by a rickety bridge without rails, then through rougher ground that climbed, finally dwindling into not much more than a path, through wild tamarind and turpentine trees, their trunks buried in tangled vine and fern. The sea was not audible or visible from here, and Billy's hooves and the wheels of her cart seemed unnecessarily noisy.

Then the road took a sharp turn to the left and ended.

She reined to a stop and looked about her.

"Lilias?"

He came out from behind one of the big turpentine trees. At first she almost did not recognize him. He was dressed in a rough workman's shirt and trousers. No ruffles, no hat, his black hair flowing in the breeze.

He came forward quickly to help her out of the cart. He lifted her gently to the ground, looked down at her.

"Let me get the cart out of sight. Just in case anyone else is interested in visiting the springs today."

He took Billy's bridle and led him, with some difficulty, farther into the woods, where he fastened the reins to a big tree, and came back to her.

"Come with me." He took her hand. "It's not far."

There was a decent path as far as the springs, which gurgled out of the ground emitting a hot, faintly medicinal odor. Then the brush grew thicker and Roderick walked ahead of her, holding bushes aside for her to pass.

The clearing had a soft grasslike covering, sprinkled with wild morning glories.

"They used to keep sheep here," Roderick said. "That's why it looks like a lawn."

Lilias stood looking around her. It was like a little room shut away from the rest of the world, like . . . she caught her breath . . . like the Garden of Eden.

Overhead the sky was cobalt blue with only traces of white clouds along the horizon.

Roderick reached for the ribbons of her bonnet.

She backed away from him.

"I shouldn't have come," she protested.

"But you did," he said matter-of-factly.

He came closer and untied the ribbons, tossed the bonnet aside. Then he ran his hands through her soft hair, scattering the pins, letting the fine locks fall to her shoulders.

She was shaking now with an emotion almost like fear, as if she had stepped too far into a dream world, so far there was no turning back.

His hand was at her throat now, then he ran his hand down inside her bodice. Was he going to rip her clothing from her? Again she drew back.

"Roderick ... I ..."

"Don't be afraid, Lilias." Then, as if he understood her feeling, he added, "This is daytime love."

He pushed the soft white material off both her shoulders, so that her breasts were revealed, white in the sunlight.

He kissed them, and kissed them again, and then, very slowly, he pulled her down on the grass.

For a long time his "daytime love" was all gentleness, his hands stroking her almost as if she were a pet kitten. Yet it seemed that all he had to do was to touch her, however lightly, and she felt the same as she had that other night, her body tingling and alive and hungry, and suddenly she flung her arms around his neck and pulled his mouth down on hers and kissed him roughly, demandingly.

He did not undress her completely. But within moments the "daytime love" had become as passionate and as violent as that night in bed and they were again locked together and the sunlight, and the soft grass and the wind in the trees were part of it. It truly was the Garden of Eden, and they were the only two beings in all the world.

She did not fall asleep afterward but lay looking up into the blue sky. The sky suddenly darkened as a shadow of a cloud across her sun. The devil's shadow? When she turned her head she found Roderick watching her.

"Thank you, my love." He was smiling.

"Thank you," she whispered.

She wished he would say more than thank you. That he would say he loved her more than anyone in the whole world, that he was going to run away with her to some place where they could always be together, like this.

And then she thought, I have been intimate with this man, more intimate than with Ian. I have given him all of myself; he has truly possessed me. And yet he is a stranger.

Slowly she pulled her dress up over her shoulders, reached to pull down her skirts.

"Happy?" he asked.

Startled, she answered, "I don't know."

"You don't know! After . . . after . . ."

"After," she repeated. "That's the trouble. After." She felt the tears coming into her eyes and covered her face with her hands.

He laughed.

"Your body is happy," he told her. "And so is mine. Never have there been two happier bodies. You can't deny that."

She took her hands from her face. "No," she said slowly. "I guess I can't. But, oh, Roderick, what are we going to do?"

"Do?" At first he looked genuinely puzzled. Then he laughed again. She did not like his laugh. It was not companionable; it was derogatory. He said, "We're going to make love, lass, as often as we can. My guts have not had enough of you, yet."

She stared at him, horrified.

"Lilias, you feel the same way. That little crotch of yours," he put his hand between her legs, "is ready to gobble me up any time, any place."

"Roderick, we can't . . ."

"Don't be stupid", he interrupted harshly." Don't say, 'we can't go on like this,' because we can, and we will."

"People will find out."

"Will they? Have you told anyone? Did anyone see me come to your house, or see you come here today?"

She shook her head. "I did see Jonathan Kincaid in front of Government House. I had a feeling he might have guessed where I was going."

"But you said nothing."

"Of course not! Jonathan is a good friend of my husband, as well as of me. He even asked me to stop by for tea at Government House on my way home."

"You do that," he said.

She looked down at her rumpled dress; ran her fingers through her tangled, tumbled hair. "How can I?"

"You can spruce up. A woman always can. I want you to have tea with Jonathan. If not to-day—" he looked at the sky, "another time. I want you to do something for me . . ." He touched the tip of one breast.

"What? What do you want me to do?"

"Jonathan's the one with all the answers down at Government House. He knows more than old Appleby about what's going on. See what's the newest on the French. How close they are."

"Why?"

"I have my reasons," he said shortly.

She remembered Rowena Gresham saying her husband was partial to the French. And Jonathan had had the same idea.

"I couldn't spy!" she cried. "I wouldn't!"

He kept his hand on her breast.

"Not even for me, my love?"

"I . . ."

"Remember what I told you could happen if you weren't good to me."

"Oh, but you wouldn't tell Ian. You were only teasing."

"What if I did tell Ian? What if he threw you out, bag and baggage? Then we could see each other any time we wanted. I'd build you a shack up in the hills with only room for a bed. Just think how wonderful it would be . . ."

"Roderick, no! No! Don't talk like that!" she cried in horror.

Suddenly he lifted her to her feet.

"Then be a good little girl and have tea with Jonathan. And ask about the French. He's sweet on you, I can tell by the way he looks at you. He'll let something drop."

She sighed. With great effort she pulled herself together, tucked her tangled hair under her bonnet, tied the bow under her chin, and started to walk through the woods.

Roderick, caught up with her, put his arm around her and walked close beside her. As they came out of the clearing next to the springs Lilias looked up at him. His eyes were warm and tender now. He said, "Don't forget you are mine. All mine."

A sound made them turn their heads. There at the springs two rough looking men were filling bottles with the hot medicinal water. They turned to stare at the couple coming out of the woods.

10.

As the *Poinciana* drifted toward the islet of Pollino, Desmond strained her eyes for her first glimpse of a Carib Indian.

Desmond never had seen a Carib; she only had heard from most people that they were cruel and lazy savages. But because of what her mother had told her she had been curious. Her Indian ancestors had not sounded like lazy savages. Cruel, perhaps, but not lazy, and not savages.

Now, through the rain, the Indians were visible on the shore. Tall men, painted with oil so that they were almost the color of boiled lobsters. Their only clothing were loin cloths that hung to the ground, their faces were garishly painted, and they were holding bows almost as tall as themselves and arrows—poisoned, she had heard, with the sap of the manchineel tree.

A canoe, made of a hollowed log, now was making its way from the beach to the *Poinciana*. One man was paddling, another standing straight and tall.

Desmond remembered her mother's description of Desmond's great grandfather, the chief, resplendent in his bright feathers and jewelry, metal ornaments called *caracolis* that hung from his ears and nose and lower lip, whenever he dressed up for an occasion.

"He was a proud man," Maria had said. "He was ashamed that his daughter, my mother, had given birth to a half-breed."

As the canoe came closer through the gray air Desmond could see the man's *caracolis*, crescent-shaped, lightly powdered with a glittering substance.

The man's face was dignified but his expression was sullen and sad. He kept one hand on a knife that hung from his loin cloth. When he spoke it was in English, but stilted and strongly accented.

"What do you want?"

He was looking up at the poop deck where Dragon was standing alone.

"Harbor for the night," Dragon called down to him.

"No." The chief shook his head.

"Only harbor in your bay, until the storm passes."

The man swept his eyes scornfully over the ship. "No," he said again. "I know who you are. I know you come to kill, to steal my food, to take my women."

"I swear that all we want is harbor."

"Leave. Now. Leave my harbor. My boats and my men are waiting with their arrows."

He started to lift his hand to give his men the signal.

"Wait!" Desmond surprised even herself. "Wait!" she called again and then ran across the deck and climbed up to stand beside Dragon.

The Indian stared at her.

"Only harbor," she told him. "No harm to you."

And she held out her hands the way she had seen her mother do, so many times.

For a moment or two the man continued to stare. Then, finally, he gave a little nod, muttered something in his own language, and signaled his oarsman to start dipping the paddle.

A cheer rose from the deck as the canoe moved away.

Dragon turned to her.

"Where did you learn that trick?"

"Trick? It's just something my mother did when she put me to bed at night."

"Your mother was a Carib?" He sounded incredulous.

Desmond shook her head. "My grandmother was."

"I see."

Ned Barnes had joined them. His ugly face still was unfriendly, but now it was suffused with sheer curiosity.

"So the lad's put you in debt . . . again."

"He has."

"You're earning your keep," Barnes told him, but his curiosity made her uncomfortable.

148

When she went through "the trick", as Dragon had called it, could she have behaved more like a girl than a boy? After all, she had been imitating her mother.

"You'll get your full share of the booty," Dragon told her. "We're all in debt to you. We could have hoisted sail and left this little bay, but we would have had to fight the storm. As it is, we can just wait, and set out for the caves the minute the wind is right."

Barnes said, "Go below, Desmond, and unclog the scuppers."

"Yes, sir!" She was glad to leave him; she was glad about the booty. She was willing to do all sorts of work, with that reward in mind.

The next morning when the rain stopped, and the wind switched up brisk and bright from the opposite direction, the sails were unfurled. With a whopping and a yaw-awing the ship was turned away from the wind, the sails veered round and the *Poinciana* sailed forth, set in another course, toward Cabra, swooping and skimming like a bird in the air.

They circled the island to the small bay that was close to the caves. Desmond recognized the spot where the distillery was located; she even caught a glimpse of the distillery and Obie's house. If they had been closer she would have waved. She wished now there were some way she could let Obie know how well she was far-ing, except for that one beating, and how she was going to get her share of the booty.

Quietly the ship slipped inside the bay and dropped sails and anchor. They went ashore a few at a time. Only old Bombo and one other man were left aboard, to be taken ashore later, before everything had been distributed.

The heavier chests and bundles of gold brick went first; Desmond was one of the last to pick up two fairly small bags, throw them over her shoulder, and climb down to a boat.

Inside the caves several torches had been propped between rocks. The ground was damp, but they were there at the right time, for the tide was out. The torches cast shadows on the walls, enormous black figures moving about on the walls and ceiling. The rocks themselves were roughhewn monsters, gargoyles and predatory birds frozen in place.

Dragon and Barnes and two of the other men began opening chests and bags and spreading out the contents.

Desmond watched, more breathlessly than she had other times, because this time, this time! she would get her full share.

Before the actual distribution began two of the men who had left the ship first, came into the cave and began passing around bottles for everyone to take a swallow. Desmond started to shake her head but the fellow holding the bottle said, "It's from the springs. It's not rum.

It's good for you," and so she took a sip of what tasted like medicine.

Dragon was at the far end of the pile and Barnes was at the end close to Desmond. One of the men passing a bottle stopped close to the quartermaster.

"We saw her, Ned," he said in a low voice.

Her. Desmond pricked up her ears.

"Who?" Barnes asked.

"The vixen. She was at the springs with her husband. If she'd been alone . . . "

Barnes nodded. "There'll come a time, Foxy. We'll talk about it. Not now." He gave a look in Dragon's direction.

"Right."

She guessed they must be talking about Roderick Gresham and the dreadful wife who had poisoned part of their crew. They were planning something they didn't want Dragon to know about. She pretended to stare at the pile of booty. But there was no point in listening any more, as they had suddenly stopped talking and Barnes was ordering them to line up against the walls of the cave.

Everyone squatted down as the treasures were handed out under Dragon's direction. They had called him fair and he was, meticulously so.

First came the money. All kinds of money—*doubloons, louis-d'ors, guineas, pieces of eight, double guineas, moidores* and *sequins*. Then came the bars of gold, and last of all, the small chests were opened and bits of clothing were distributed.

Dragon directed the operation. Ned distributed money, and then goods. Sometimes Dragon would specify to whom an article should be given. When Barnes dropped coins into Desmond's bag he gave her a disdainful look. His dislike was more than evident, but Desmond could look across the cave and see that Dragon was keeping his eye on the quartermaster.

Ned practically threw a pair of earrings in her direction. Emeralds bound with silver, the most beautiful things she ever had seen. But there was no way to wear them; her ears had not been pierced. Regretfully she dropped them into her bag. Some day, some day! With her hair grown long and piled high, those emeralds would dangle from her ears.

It was funny to see the men pouncing on plumed hats, on wigs, even pulling stockings on over their hairy legs. Not to mention jewelry. Sparkling necklaces were draped over their rough shirts, and since their ears were pierced, the fashion amongst most pirates, earrings dangled from their ears. Barnes tried to hang two on his one ear, which caused the men to double up with laughter. They all bounded about and pummeled one another like children.

While Barnes was busy with his clowning, Dragon crossed the cave to Desmond. In his hand was a necklace made of carved gold pieces.

"This should help you get rich." He dangled the necklace in front of her eyes.

"Oh, thank you! It's beautiful!" she cried.

"More to the point, it's valuable."

She slipped the necklace over her head and longed for a looking glass. She let the necklace lie against her bare throat inside the open collar of her old shirt. It was cold and heavy but immensely satisfying; she never had had a necklace before. She stood up, enjoying it, unconsciously lifting her chin, as if she were completely dressed up.

For a moment Dargon looked down at her, an odd half-smile on his face, and then he turned away abruptly.

She put her fingers against the carved gold pieces. She closed her eyes and tried to pretend she was wearing a dress, and Dragon, instead of being amused, was admiring her.

She heard a laugh. Then, "Hey, look at the boy!"

Cruikshank grabbed her arm and dragged her in front of one of the flaming torches. He was a big black man; his size was awesome.

"Pretty hoity-toity, there!" He grinned his toothy grin.

"Look at the gold nuggets!" Romley added.

"Look at him, proud as a peacock."

"Naw, he's primping, like lady what's-her-name."

Lady Desmond suddenly slipped back down on the floor. Slowly she took the necklace from her throat and dropped it in the money bag where she had put the earrings. She had been behaving like a woman. She must be careful.

Soon there was the long process of carrying the booty back to the ship each man clutching his own share. Desmond took hers back to the corner beside her hammock.

When she came back out onto the deck she found everyone busy drinking rum. She accepted a small coconut shell of the fiery liquid, just so she would not be conspicuous, sipped it carefully, then went to find Bombo and his lime and sugar mixture to put with the rum.

"Happy, boy?" the old man asked, as he poured into her cup.

"Yes."

"You're quite a hero."

She smiled, embarrassedly.

The men would be getting drunk soon, she was sure. She wanted to hide away, she dreaded their attention, dreaded being a hero.

Romley, now wearing a wig and a plumed hat that looked ludicrous with his grimy beard and pug nose, swung over to where Bombo and Desmond were talking.

"Coming with us, boy?" he asked.

"Where?"

"To town, of course, with our pockets full of gold."

"I don't . . . she started to protest but now another man had joined them.

"Course he's coming, he wouldn't miss it. This lad's a game one."

"Maybe he doesn't want to go," Bombo said quietly, his eyes on Desmond.

Romley grabbed her arm.

"Of course he's coming. There'll be more rum and plenty of good grub . . . you're kind of skinny, boy. And," he winked, "there'll be girls. There's sure to be girls. We'll find one for you about your size, Monkey."

"Monkey? I thought his name was Desmond," Bombo said.

"Monkey's better. That's what we'll call him. Grab your doubloons, Monkey, and come along!"

Big black Cruikshank grabbed her other arm.

"You'll have a good time," Bombo assured her.

Desmond looked around helplessly. Where was Dragon? She felt sure Dragon would help her. But he was no place in sight.

Romley and Cruikshank let go of her. "Go get your money, and quick, or I'll come after you," Romley told her.

After they got ashore there was a long walk to town.

It was easy to keep up with the others because their walk was uncertain. They paid little

155

attention to her; they were busy laughing and singing snatches of songs:

. . . but one man of her crew alive, what put to sea with seventy-five . . .
. . . drink and the devil had done for the rest . . . "Yo ho, yo ho, to Edwardsville we go. Get out the rum for here we come, Yo ho, yo ho! Fill up the glasses, bring out the lasses, Yo ho, Yo ho!"

The stormy weather was over; the moon was coming out to jump in and out behind clouds, alternately illuminating the sea on one side of the road and the hills on the other. In a way she was excited to be going along; she had not been in a town since she left home, and back on Barbados she never had had money in her pockets. Perhaps there would be something to buy besides rum and food.

Edwardsville was a tiny village but it did have two taverns. They decided to stop at the first one they reached, THE BILLY GOAT. The sign with its horns was silhouetted in the moonlight.

There were a few customers who looked up with annoyed and frightened faces when the pirates burst in.

The Billy Goat was a large low room, with bright red curtains at its windows and a floor cleanly sanded. The air was blue with tobacco smoke.

Some of the pirates sat down at tables and pounded on them for service. Others went up close to the seated customers crying out, "Have a drink with us!" less affably than threateningly.

At least they seemed to have forgotten about Desmond. She sat in a corner, digging her hands into her pockets and holding tightly to her money. She did not order anything to drink.

Slowly some of their gaiety began to change color, to be spotted with sharp tones and rebuffs, small arguments threatening to erupt any moment into something serious.

"Girl, I want a girl," Freedman mumbled. "Come on, Monkey, let's find us girls."

It was the first time any of them had spoken to her since they came into the tavern.

"There are girls in the other tavern," Foxy said.

"But it's dark."

"All the better! They're all black on this island. But they're ready and willing and right tasty."

"Me, I like black meat." Cruikshank chuckled.

Desmond was beginning to feel like a scared child. One side of her they were talking about girls, on the other two of the pirates were berating one of the regular customers for not drinking with them, finally jumping to their feet with knives in their hands, knocking over the table with a great crash, bottles flying.

When Freedman and Foxy got to their feet and moved toward the door, Desmond followed. Outside in the dark she determined to run away from them, to go back to the ship, however difficult it might be. The *Poinciana* had become home. There she felt much safer than here on land with all these drunken men.

Thank God they did not see her follow them, and when she glanced back over her shoulder at the doorway she did not see anyone watching her.

There were only a few dim lights along Edwardsville's one street. She leaned against the stone wall of the tavern and watched the others stagger along that street.

When they had disappeared, she moved out into the street herself, again thankful because they were walking in the opposite direction from the road that led to the ship.

It would be a long walk and she was already tired. She wished it were daylight now so that Edwardsville's few stores would be open. She only passed one and it seemed to be a combination of food and general merchandise, nothing as grand as the stores she remembered from Barbados. Well, there would be another ship capture, another distribution of loot, another island, another town. There might even be a place where she could sneak away and buy girl's clothes.

Barbados. What if they reached there? Would her mother forgive her for running away if she came home with presents? Would her mother believe how she had gotten them?

The lights began to grow fewer. When the moon came out from behind the clouds she moved quickly, almost running, along the road, sometimes stumbling over rocks. When the moon was obscured she slowed her pace.

She felt very alone, but not completely unhappy. After all, she had proved her worth in more than one way, she was no longer poor, and she seemed to be getting away with her masquerade as a boy.

Also, as she walked, she thought about Dragon.

He was definitely the leader. It was obvious that the others were in awe of him—except, of course, Ned Barnes.

She had never known anyone like Dragon.

They said he was fair, and he was. And he had been kind to her. But, after all, he was the captain of a pirate ship. He *was* a pirate. He would be capable of cruelty. What would he be like if he found out she was a girl? In a way she wished he did know.

Now she heard horse's hooves and the creak of wheels. She drew back to the bushes at the side of the road, listening to the approaching vehicle. The sky was clouded over at that moment and perhaps no one would spot her there.

But just as the sound grew louder, the moon abruptly appeared, shining full in her face.

The carriage stopped.

There was no reason to be afraid, of course. She had instinctively tried to hide because she was still in the mood of escape. But all she needed to do was to say good evening and go on her way.

It was a man alone in the carriage. She could not make out his face.

"Hallo, there," he called out.

"Hallo."

"You want a ride to town?"

"No, thank you. I'm just going back to my ship."

"The harbor is in the other direction."

"My ship isn't."

He was getting out of the carriage now and she began to be afraid as he moved closer to her in her spot of bright moonlight.

He was a big man. His shape and his posture began to seem familiar. She could just see the long curly hair under his big hat. Then she remembered. It was the man who had come to the distillery for rum; it was the husband of the woman the pirates had talked about. What was his name? Roderick Gresham, the richest planter on the island.

"Who are you and where are you going?" he asked,

"I'm Desmond Duval and my ship is the *Poinciana* and it's anchored by the caves."

160

"Pirate ship."

"Yes." What would he do? Arrest her? Force her to come to town?

He laughed. "Pirates are pretty young these days. All right. Run along."

But as she started to turn away, he reached out and grabbed her arm, put his face closer to hers and stared, letting his eyes run down her body.

"Wait a minute." She didn't like his smile. "I've seen you before."

11.

Lilias was frightened by the men at the springs, but Roderick kept his arm around her shoulders and led her past.

"Who were they?" she asked. "Do you know them? Did you recognize them?"

He shook his head. "The springs are not on my property. Anyone is free to visit them. They look like privateers to me. Sometimes they put in down by the caves. Pay no attention."

Had she known such ruffians might be about she would have been afraid to drive up here alone. But she should have remembered the story of Mrs. Gresham and the poisoning. Had she really done it? Lilias did not want to ask Roderick; she did not want even to remember that he had a wife.

When they got to the cart he helped her in, then he reached up and took both her hands and held them firmly.

"You will help me, won't you, Lilias? If you do, I shall make you the happiest woman in the world."

His eyes gripped her as firmly as his hands.

"But Jonathan is a friend of mine," she protested.

"Am I not a dearer friend?"

"Oh, Roderick!" She turned her head away.

"It is your turn to send a message . . . when you are ready to see me." His lips curled into an amused smile, then he said, "But don't try. Until you have talked to Jonathan Kincaid. Until you have something to tell me." He let go of her hands, stepped forward and slapped Billy across the rump. The cart started moving and she had to grab the reins.

She let the donkey hurry her through the woods, but when she was closer to town she slowed him down.

She felt as if there were two women riding side by side in that donkey cart. One was the animal creature who had succumbed so easily to Roderick. But the other woman was Ian's wife. And it was Ian's wife who thought that if she did do what Roderick asked, it would not be doing something for Roderick, it would be because of his threat to go to Ian.

But would he? She did not really believe he would. Yet the bare possibility was frightening.

It was later than she had guessed. The sun was already slowly going down. They had spent more time there in that grassy field than she had realized. It would be much too late today to have tea with Jonathan.

Edwardsville's street was practically deserted as the cart clattered along. Government House

163

was on the edge of town on the way home. The front doors were closed when she reached it, the iron gate in place. She gave a sigh of relief at her reprieve for the moment. It would have to be another day.

She was tired as she drove up into the hills. The sun was sinking into the channel now, casting rosy shadows on the dark blue water and on the piles of white clouds along the horizon. She urged Billy to go a little faster, to get her home before the quick darkness entirely enveloped the island. Then, just as she swung around a corner she saw ahead of her a man sitting on a donkey, beside the road.

She could not turn around and go back. Go back where? There was nothing to do but go forward and hope it was a harmless stranger that she would have to pass.

Her hands shook on the reins. She remembered the two men at the springs. But surely no privateer would be this far up in the hills, nor would he be riding a donkey.

She was almost holding her breath as she drew closer to the silent figure. And then, when she was only a few feet away, she recognized Jonathan's erect posture.

She drew up beside him and stopped.

"Jonathan . . ." she almost stammered, in relief as well as surprise. "I'm sorry I was too late for tea."

He smiled. "You are forgiven."

Tea would have been stuffy, he thought. *I*

164

would have been pretending I was just a friend of the family, just wanting to straighten out her life. And she would have gone on being the prim little wife. Things are different when it starts to get dark. She is really distraught tonight, as she pretended to be over thunder that afternoon. She'll be looking for comfort again. And I shall give it to her.

"Jonathan, what are you doing way out here?"

"Waiting for you."

"Waiting for me?" Her eyes widened.

"I just wanted to make sure you got home safely." His voice was dry.

"I see." But she was still wide-eyed.

"May I escort you the rest of the way?"

"Of course."

But she felt awkward, almost the way she would have felt if it had been Ian there at the side of the road, worrying about her safety. She drove slowly, hearing the other donkey's feet clumping along beside the cart.

It was completely dark before they reached the house and she was glad because her disheveled appearance would not be so evident. When they came into the candlelit living room she could smell the food Zula was cooking in the kitchen.

"You'll stay for dinner?" she asked Jonathan.

"What would people say?"

"Oh, Jonathan!" She was sure she was blushing. "I'll go tell Zula to set another place. Please make yourself comfortable."

When she came back from the kitchen Jonathan had sat down near a candle with her old copy of *Pilgrim's Progress*. She excused herself again and hurried into her bedroom.

She ran to her mirror. Even by candlelight she could see that she was pale, that strands of unpinned hair were slipping from her bonnet. She hurried to change, slipped out of her rumpled dress, washed her face thoroughly, grabbed another frock, a modest gray linsey-woolsey, then brushed her hair vigorously and combed it carefully into place, thankful that there was a new packet of hairpins in her dresser drawer. She felt more composed now, more like Mrs. Everett, the parson's wife. But when she came back into the living room to face Jonathan's sharp blue eyes, some of her discomfiture returned. She was not sure how she could slip into easy conversation.

Jonathan closed the book in his hands. "Bunyan is always good to dip into. He knew how to dramatize religion."

Lilias nodded absently. "Would you like some sherry?" she asked.

"Ian's precious sherry? Saved for weddings and funerals?"

"I'm tired from driving. I'd like a little sherry."

"You drove a long way?"

"Yes," she answered shortly.

She turned her head and he studied her profile. Where had she gone? What had she been up to that afternoon? There was guilt written all over her face. He would swear she had had some sort of rendezvous, but with whom? Roderick Gresham? She was ready for a dalliance, but her nervous manner made him suspect that again she had resisted succumbing. To whomever it was.

"I don't suppose you'd like to tell me where you took your long drive?"

"What does it matter? What business is it of yours where I go or what I do?"

Anger again. That surprising temper.

"I suppose it is none of my business," he said quietly. "Yes, I would like a glass of sherry. Where is it? And may I pour?"

"In the cupboard there." She pointed, then sat down in a chair in one of the shadowy corners.

A moment later he had brought her one of the tiny glasses and poured one for himself. He lifted his, as if he were making a toast, and they both sipped.

"You're not only tired tonight, Lilias, you're nervous," he said, after a moment.

"Am I?"

"You are. What's the matter?"

"Nothing. Nothing at all." Her answer came a bit too quickly.

"You're not a very good liar, Lilias."

"Jonathan will you please stop pecking away

at me? I'm tired, and I'm not used to entertaining when Ian's away."

"Are you worried about what he will say?"

"Of course not! Not at all. I'm sure he will be pleased at your seeing me home. I'm sure he would have wanted me to ask you to stay to dinner. It's not a special dinner at all. Just one of Zula's usual concoctions; she's not very imaginative, you know, and of course I scarcely know how to boil water. But after you came all the way up here I'm sure he wouldn't want you to go away hungry and I am glad of the company, I really am." She knew she was rambling but seemed unable to stop herself.

"That was quite a speech." Jonathan's eyes were twinkling. "Didn't you get out of breath?"

"I'm sorry!"

"For what?"

"For rattling on like that." *Why doesn't he stop?*

"No need to apologize. I quite understand."

She bristled a little and took a larger swallow of her sherry. "Understand what?"

"You. When a woman talks like that, rambling on about nothing at all."

"What do you mean?"

"You mean, what does *it* mean. It means she has something else she would like to say but is afraid to talk about. What is it, Lilias? I am your friend. You can confide in me."

"I tell you, there is nothing to confide!" Her voice was sharper than she intended.

"You mean there's nothing you *want* to confide. So be it."

How much did Jonathan know? Or guess? She could not be sure. At any rate, she must be nice to Jonathan. Placate him so by no chance would he voice his suspicions—if he had suspicions—to Ian. As she must placate Roderick with government house information. She must pull herself together and behave normally, not just talk, talk, talk.

She looked up. Thank goodness Zula was coming in from the kitchen carrying a big iron pot.

"Jonathan, dinner is served." She put her empty glass on the table beside her and stood up.

Conversation limped along at the dinner table. Zula had made a mutton stew which was spicy, and a bit tough. And there were pickled beet roots and gherkins. The most that could be said for the meal was that it was nourishing.

"I do miss English cooking," Lilias said. "My Aunt Rachel has such a wonderful cook. She has been with the family forever and she knows just how to make Yorkshire pudding, for instance. Not to mention all the wonderful other side dishes."

Jonathan nodded. "I miss it, too. Almost as much as I miss the theater, and the newspapers. Sometimes I feel that I'm not in a real world, as if I had been spirited away to an imaginary island, like Sir Francis Bacon's *The*

New Atlantis. I shall be so happy when I go back to that real world, where I know what's happened soon after it's happened instead of not knowing for months."

This was her chance, of course, to try to find out what was going on, right here in the West Indies. But how to begin? She had always waved away any talk of war; she had behaved like the innocent child-woman who does not want to know about unpleasant possibilities. Somehow, now, she must find a way to appear interested. The burden was a heavy one. She was unhappy just remembering Roderick and his threat.

They were silent during the pineapple and goat cheese dessert. Now and then Jonathan would give her a thoughtful glance. Meanwhile Lilias was doing her best to think of some way to question him. There should be brandy in the house, so perhaps she could ply him with liquor, to loosen his tongue. On the other hand, she never had seen Jonathan the least bit tipsy. He was an efficient, self-controlled man, always in command of himself.

Jonthan sat down on the settee and got out his pipe and she brought him the bowl. He smiled up at her as she handed it to him, the same quizzical quirk of a smile he had given her that Sunday afternoon, just before he left. That was something to remember; that was a clue to how she should behave. She guessed that Jonathan was smitten with her. She bent and lightly kissed the top of his head before she turned away and sat down opposite him.

She saw the surprised look on his face, but he said nothing; just sat there puffing on his pipe and watching her.

After awhile Zula appeared in the doorway. "Is there anything else you want, mistress?"

"No, I think not, Zula."

"Then I shall bid you good night and go to my quarters."

"Good night, Zula."

Jonathan repeated after her, "Good night, Zula," with a lilt in his voice.

When the door closed on Zula Jonathan put down his pipe and smiled across at Lilias.

"So here we are, alone again."

"Now, Jonathan, don't start talking that way."

"I promise you, dear lady, I shall not approach you until you give me a signal indicating your willingness. I am no rapist."

Her body still tingled, still burned from Roderick's caresses. She could not imagine responding to Jonathan. And yet she must not be angry with him. She must placate him, she must make him trust her, if she would do what she had to do: get him to talk.

"Come over and sit beside me, Lilias. You're nervous and upset, in need of comfort. God knows why. But it doesn't matter. I shan't probe."

She hesitated. Then, after a moment she

crossed the room and sat down beside him. He put one arm, lightly across her shoulders.

"Relax my dear. Put your head on my shoulder and feel safe." His voice was quiet and comforting.

For a long while neither of them spoke.

A breeze was stirring the shutters through which the moonlight slanted, a breeze that set the candles dancing. There was no sound but the tree toads chirping, and the night birds calling out to each other with infrequent trills.

Lilias began slowly, reaching for each word.

"Jonathan, I was just thinking of what you said about our being so far away from the real world. Are we, really? Sometimes I am so afraid!"

"As you are afraid of thunder?" he teased.

"Oh, more than that. Much more!"

She tried to turn on her most innocent expression, as if she were a child trying her best to join in an adult conversation.

Jonathan stroked her shoulder gently. Finally he said, "If you want the truth, we are not far away from danger. Far away from the high commands, from decisions, but, on the other hand, the Caribbean is one of the battlefields. For whatever war is going on. Of course, sometimes there is still fighting here after peace has been declared. The Spanish have gone on being enemies for over a hundred years after the defeat of the Spanish Armada."

Talk, talk, talk, she thought. *What about now? What is the situation here, now?*

She tried, "But now it is the French we are fighting."

"And they are fighting us," Jonathan added.

She must ask, she must learn! Something about now, right now, for Roderick!

"Do you think the French will come to Cabra?"

"Yes."

She stiffened. More in excitement than in fear, because this was the sort of thing she wanted to find out about.

Jonathan held her closer. "No need to be afraid, Lilias. Of course they want Cabra. For its strategic position here on the channel. But I don't think they will take it."

"Why not?" she asked ingenuously.

"We have ways of knowing things at Government House. Ships flying friendly flags deliver messages from time to time."

"What kind of messages?" She snuggled closer to him, felt his hand cover one of her breasts. She should have pulled away, but she did not try. He was talking now.

"I'm speaking out of school if I tell you anything."

Her breast was stiffening under his hand. Was she giving him a signal, after all?

"Jonathan, you're not speaking out of school, to me. You're just . . . comforting me, making me feel safe. What kind of a message?"

Jonathan was close beside her. His other hand was on her other breast.

"This much I can tell you, my sweet. Governor Appleby has ordered reinforcements. They should arrive any day now. Does that make you feel safe?"

She sighed. "Oh, yes!" She had the information now, for Roderick.

"Let's talk about happier things, sweetheart. Such as what you have been doing to amuse yourself since you have learned to drive."

She mumbled, "Just having the cart and being able to go out any time I want is a joy in itself. Tomorrow I go back to the dressmaker for fittings."

Tomorrow, she thought, *I must find Roderick*.

"Talk, talk. Women talk too much." Suddenly both his arms were around her and he had pulled her tight against him, his mouth over hers.

There was no response. She pulled her face away, she struggled to free herself from his arms.

"Stop it, Jonathan! Stop it!" She finally broke away and stood beside him. "You must not do this to me!

He reached out to grab her but she slapped him across the face.

"You asked for it," he told her, rubbing his cheek.

"I did not!"

"You damned well did ask for it. Snuggling up beside me like a kitten, playing the suductress to the hilt. Teasing. You are the one who should be slapped."

She burst into tears and buried her face in her hands.

He was distressed to see her in tears but he did not know what to say, or to do. He was as furious with himself as he was with her.

"I'm leaving now."

She took her hands from her tear-stained face.

"Yes. Please go."

"You shan't see me again until Ian is home. I hope that will be soon."

"So do I!"

"I wonder if he'll notice." His voice was sarcastic.

"Notice what?"

"How you've changed, Mrs. Everett. And not for the better."

He turned and left.

12.

When Roderick Gresham said, "I've seen you before," Desmond tried to jerk her arm free but he held her firmly.

"Let me go! I must get back to my ship!"

"You were bathing, naked, in the bay at the rum distillery, weren't you?"

"No!"

"Obie lied. He told me there was no girl at his place, the rascal."

"There wasn't!"

To her surprise he let go of her arm, dropped it as if it were distasteful.

"You need a bath, you little slut."

Desmond tossed her head angrily and began running down the road. He was right behind her, his longer legs giving him the advantage. He soon caught up with her and grabbed her by the shoulders. He swung her around facing him.

"I *saw* you. Naked as a jaybird, coming out of the water."

"Let go of me!" One hand went to the cutlass hanging from her belt. "I warn you, if you don't let me go, I'll swing this!"

His eyes were shining in the moonlight. He laughed. "You little devil, you would't dare!"

"I would!"

"You've got spirit. I like that." He let go of her and smiled down at her.

"Now listen to me. You're coming with me down to the beach for that bath you need and then . . ."

As he reached for her again she swung the cutlass toward his outreaching arm, and then turned and again started running down the road.

He was right behind her, swearing under his breath. He caught up with her around a curve where ancient trees partially blotted out the moonlight. At the end of the curve Desmond darted into the bushes, hoping he would not see her, hoping she could hide there until he had given up the chase.

But he was closer than she had realized. He was close enough behind her to see where she had gone.

He caught up with her. This time he grabbed both her arms and held them in a vise like grip.

"Where the hell do you think you're going?"

"To my ship."

"Not yet you're going to that ship. Not quite yet."

He threw her down on her back and wrenched her cutlass away from her grasp.

She started to scream. He knelt beside her, and put one hand around her throat.

"No need to scream, you little bitch. No one would hear you," he said harshly.

He took his hand away from her throat. She swallowed painfully.

"No," he said, "you will do exactly what I tell you. Do you understand? It's not every night I find a tender morsel along the highway and I mean to have you."

He was astraddle of her now, holding her arms up above her head, bending his open mouth toward hers. She twisted her face to one side and then the other, avoiding him, but it was no use: his tongue had found her mouth.

He let go of her arms and reached for her trousers. She struck at both sides of his head and he let out an angry groan.

He moved off of her, struggling to undo her trousers. She began kicking at his groin and he groaned again. And then she screamed, louder than before.

Gresham was still groaning and swearing under his breath when they both heard footsteps thumping along the road.

Desmond called out at the top of her lungs, "Help! Help!"

The footsteps stopped.

"Who's there?"

It was Dragon's voice!

"Dragon! Dragon!" she shouted.

He burst through the bushes as Desmond and Gresham both staggered to their feet.

She stumbled over to Dragon's side, looked

up at him in gratitude, longing to throw her arms around his neck.

Dragon was not looking at her, but at Roderick. The two men stood there in silence.

Then Roderick laughed. He said, "Well, well, well."

"What were you doing to the boy?"

Roderick laughed again.

Now Dragon turned to Desmond. "What happened?"

"I was trying to go back to the ship. He stopped me."

"That's her story," Roderick said.

"*Her* story?"

"She's no boy. I've seen her stark naked, stepping out of the ocean like a mermaid with legs."

"It's not true!" Desmond cried. "He's lying."

Dragon looked at her. "I'll get you back to your ship," he said gruffly. "Come along."

He took her arm and led her back to the road; they walked away with Roderick's laughter ringing in their ears. Neither spoke until Dragon asked, not looking in her direction, "What was he trying to do to you, Desmond? Why did you scream?"

"He slapped me. He called me dirty names. He ..."

Had Dragon believed Roderick when he said she was a girl? Would he ask her? Would she be able to go on lying?

If he believed Roderick Gresham, then he

would know what Gresham had been trying to do to her. She stared straight ahead into the night, not wanting to face Dragon.

Dragon said, rather dryly, "I guess you're lucky I came along."

"More than lucky." She smoothed at her tangled hair, she rubbed the back of her hand across her mouth to wipe away the memory of that awful kiss. She wondered if her arms were bruised from the way Roderick had held them.

"You went to town with the others, didn't you, Desmond? Why were you coming back alone? Didn't you have a good time?"

"No, I didn't. I don't like drinking. And I didn't want to go after girls the way they did."

"If you felt that way, why did you go to town?"

"They made me go!" she cried, then added, in a lower, apologetic tone, "I was afraid not to."

Dragon said, in an equally low tone, "You're not as brave as you pretend to be, are you?"

She could not answer that.

They came over the brow of a little hill. Below them they could see the *Poinciana*, anchored in the moonlit bay. Desmond started to walk a little faster.

"Wait a minute."

She turned around. Dragon was standing still.

"Desmond, before we go back to the ship I'd like to talk to you."

She swallowed. "Yes, sir!"

"Had you known that man I found you with before?"

"No, sir."

"He said he had seen you before. Had you seen him?"

"Yes. I know who he is. Roderick Gresham, the richest planter on Cabra. His wife . . ." She faltered.

"What about his wife?"

"She . . . they say she poisoned some of your crew."

"Yes."

"That was wicked! Desmond cried. "She is wicked, and he is wicked, too."

"And a liar?"

"Yes!"

"Are you a liar now, Desmond?"

"No, I am not! I don't know why he said I am a girl. He must be drunk, or crazy," she said stoutly.

The *Poinciana* was right below the hill, and she started running toward it. Halfway down Dragon caught up with her.

"Desmond! Stop!"

He did not touch her; he did not need to, his voice was that of the captain of the ship, and she obeyed. She turned around. He was looking down at her with those enormous clear eyes. Even in the moonlight she could feel them.

"Are you a girl, Desmond?"

This time she did not protest aloud; she did

not even answer. She knew he had guessed the truth.

Then he smiled.

"Oh, Dragon," she pleaded, "please, don't tell anybody! Not anybody! When they found out on that other ship, it was dreadful. That was why I had to jump overboard and run away!"

Dragon's face did not change expression. He said quietly, "Let's sit down, Desmond. Let's begin at the beginning." He pointed to two large rocks on the edge of the path.

"The beginning?"

"Who you really are, where you really came from."

"But I told you!"

"Wait a minute. Remember when I said I thought you were gently born? I guess that was what it was, because your gestures were those of a woman."

"Oh, I never thought!"

They were seated now, only a few feet apart. The moon was directly above them, like a great round torch in the sky.

"And when I saw you with that necklace," Dragon went on, "I began to wonder just what kind of 'boy' you were. Again, your gestures were feminine."

"I see." She sighed.

He said, "You ran away from that other ship because you were afraid of the men. You went

182

to town tonight because you were afraid not to go. Aren't you afraid of me?"

She looked at him sharply. Was he, after all, just another man? Would he turn on her, the way young Alan Forrester had? Alan had been her playmate, she had known him all her life; she had trusted him. They had wrestled together and teased each other and dared each other to do all sorts of childish feats like climbing rotten trees or holding one's breath under water. But that last night, that awful night, he had been a different Alan.

She started to get up from the rock.

Dragon was immediately beside her. He put his hands on her shoulders and looked down at her.

"I'm a man, too, Desmond."

He ran his hand from her shoulder gently down across one breast.

She caught her breath.

"But you are kind," she stammered. "Like Obie was."

He took his hand away.

"Obie? Obediah Jackson?"

"Yes. He found me on the beach and he took me in and took care of me. And then let me work for him, as if I were a boy. I hated it when your men took me away."

"But you would have been safe."

"I'll be safe as long as nobody knows I'm a girl."

"I think that will become increasingly difficult." His voice was dry. Again he touched her breast. "What are we going to do about you? You can't go on playing pirate. You've got to find some other way of life. It's all wrong for you to be aboard the *Poinciana.* You know that, don't you?"

"Where else in the world can I go?"

"Home," he suggested.

"No! Never! I won't be a slave, just because I'm a girl!"

"No need for you to be a slave."

"It's the same thing. My own mother told me no man ever would marry me. I'm a nobody. I'm a bastard and I'm part Indian and I'd have to be what that man called me tonight. A slut. It's the same as being a slave in a man's world."

"You're good-looking and you're brave. That's all that matters."

Good-looking. Brave. He sounded as if he meant it. If a woman were good-looking and brave, would she be all right in a man's world?

Impulsively she flung her arms around his neck.

"Oh, Dragon, don't send me away! Don't make me leave the *Poinciana!*"

Don't make me leave you, she was thinking. *I want to stay with you and help you when a ship is captured. I want to be us together fighting and celebrating afterward.*

Her breasts were pushed against him as she kissed him. He could feel his organ swelling.

Then they looked into each other's eyes, without speaking.

He took her by the hand and led her down the path to the beach and along the beach around a short peninsula, out of sight from the ship. Again he put his hand on her breast, felt it stiffen and rise.

"Desmond, would you please take off that ugly shirt?"

Desmond, thought: *I would do anything he asked me to. Anything!*

She undid the buttons, and slipped her arms out of the sleeves as Dragon took it from her.

"Beautiful!" he whispered. "Beautiful!"

Her breasts were young and firm and white in the moonlight, in contrast to the tan of her face and throat, the nipples pink and tender. He kissed one and then the other, watched her trembling; he put his hands around her slender waist and held her.

"Desmond, have you ever made love?"

She shook her head.

"You've never been with a man?"

She frowned. She didn't want to tell him; she was ashamed of what happened back in the Forrester woods on Barbados. But he had to know! She bit her lip, then buried her head against his chest.

"There was a boy, back on Barbados," she said into his shirt. "We'd grown up together, played together. We were friends. Even if he was the master's son and I was only a slave's

185

child. And then one night . . . I thought we were just wrestling, as we had before. But he forced me down. He hurt me dreadfully. It wasn't making love. It wasn't making love, at all!"

"Of course not."

"Oh, Dragon, I am so ashamed!"

"Desmond, look at me."

She lifted her tear-strewn face.

"I will show you what love is, my darling."

He picked her up and carried her to a level stretch of beach, where he gently laid her down.

He unfastened the buttons on her pantaloons and pulled them off. He lay down beside her and kissed her lips, her breasts, while his gentle hands roamed her body. She murmured with happiness.

She lay there trembling while he pulled off his jacket and trousers. His body was long and lean, his penis upright, quivering as her whole self was quivering.

He parted her legs and stroked her, slowly, steadily, until it was as if a new pulse had been created. She arched her knees as he moved across her and entered her and she cried out as the rhythm of the completeness began.

Afterward they lay there with their arms around each other. Silence. The moonlight. The only sounds were the lapping of the waves along the beach and the beating of their two hearts.

Like an intrusion from another world the new sounds came to them. A jumble of loud voices and singing and the heavy tromp of feet, in the distance.

The men were coming back to the ship.

He helped her to her feet.

"We must go, too, my darling."

They dressed without speaking and hurried back to the path.

They could see the men in the distance, now.

"Dragon!" she cried, "promise me you won't tell them I'm a girl. Not even Barnes! Promise? They'll all be after me!"

Dragon looked down at her. "Of course I promise!"

"Oh, Dragon, it was wonderful!"

"It *was* wonderful. But right now, start acting . . . like a boy."

His words were a stern command. Only his soft eyes betrayed him.

13.

Lilias did have an appointment with the dress-maker for the next day. She knew it was a chance to go to town, perhaps to meet Roderick and tell him what little she had learned from Jonathan. But the memory of the magic of Roderick's touch was fading. She was beginning to feel as if she had had a disease. She had allowed her body to rule her. No longer did she feel like the two women riding side by side in that cart. She was becoming only Mrs. Everett now.

She would be disloyal to Jonathan by reporting the news about the French ship and the local reinforcements. But it was not the fortunes of war that bothered her, it was the perhaps illogical fear that Roderick would let Ian know, in some way, about their relationship. This she must prevent.

She went to town but there was no sign of Roderick anywhere; she returned home relieved, yet disappointed.

She was inexperienced in this sort of game. Alone she pondered for a day or so, and finally decided to write him a note saying no more than "I have something to tell you," and take it with her in her reticule, in the hopes of meeting Roderick, or of finding someone who could deliver the message.

Again she went to the general store and bought some more material and again she went to the dressmaker's. Madame Collette was a wonderful excuse for frequent trips to Edwardsville.

She was in the back room when the bell in the front tinkled and Madame Collette excused herself.

From the other side of the curtain Lilias could recognize the voice. Rowena Gresham's, rasping with cold conceit. The dressmaker was to come to her house the next day. Something about clothes for the children. She insisted upon it, even if it meant closing the shop. Madame Collette asked if it would be possible for her to go out today, if Mrs. Gresham was in such a hurry, but Mrs. Gresham explained that she was on her way to tea at Government House and that the children were off for an outing, adding that she was glad not to be at home today because her husband was there, straightening out some trouble with his workmen. "Most unpleasant."

Lilias, listening to every word, thought: *this is my chance. It will only take a moment to tell him; I can pretend I am calling on Mrs. Gresham and am disappointed not to find her at home.*

When the dressmaker came back Lilias lis-

189

tened impatiently to her tale of woe. Madame
Collette did not like to leave her shop, she did
not like working for Mrs. Gresham, things had
been different back on Martinique, even if she
had been a slave, and so on. Lilias said nothing.

She only nodded absently when told when
her next fitting would be; she hurried out of the
shop and out on the street where she had left
the donkey cart.

Two women passing spoke to her, stopped,
ready for a cozy chat. She assured them she
was in good health, so was her husband, that
the heat did not bother her, not really. Then
she told them she was late for an errand and
dashed for the cart.

It was warm that afternoon but she really
didn't mind because she was so anxious to find
Roderick and get it over with.

She was determined to break off with him.
She must make him understand that she was
through, that she would never see him again.

One of the Gresham slaves opened the gate
for her and she drove into the yard. She was
going to drive right up to the front of the house
but the black man held up his hand signalling
her to stop. He looked up at her as she drew in
the reins.

"Mistress not home, ma'am."

"And your master?"

He shook his head. Then he pointed toward
the barn and the slave quarters.

Lilias took a deep breath.

"I'll find him," she said at last.

The man frowned and again shook his head.

For a moment Lilias considered handing this man her note and asking him to deliver it. But he was a field slave, she was sure, naked above the waist and sullen-faced. She climbed out of the cart.

As she walked slowly across the rocky uneven land in the direction of the barn, she became aware of a sound of wailing. It was not a child, nor was it an animal, it was a weird mournful repetition, almost like a chant.

What could it be?

The sound increased as she moved forward. It seemed to be coming from a spot behind the barn.

It was rather frightening, but her curiosity overcame her apprehension and she went in the direction of the rear of the barn before she looked into the open door.

The moment she had rounded the corner she could see the source of the sound.

From the branches of a big turpentine tree an iron cage was hanging. A man was lying in it, clinging to the bars with gaunt black hands and moaning, as if he were too weak to cry out for help.

The back of her hand against her mouth, Lilias looked up in horor.

"What's the matter, lady?"

She turned. Another field hand was not far away, leaning on a rake.

She could not speak.

"Ain't you never seen a man hung up to dry afore?"

"Hung up to dry . . ." She choked.

"Whipping's too good for him, Master Gresham says. He's a bad man. A thief. A robber."

She did not like the expression on this man's face. He was not shocked; he was grimly amused.

"How long must he stay there?" she asked.

The man shrugged. "Till he don't make no more noise. Till he dead."

"Mr. Gresham put him there?" she asked, not believing what she knew she would hear.

"Course he did."

Lilias felt as if she were going to be sick. She turned and ran back around the barn. Ahead of her, as she ran, came the sound of screaming, and when she reached the barn door she could see what it was. Inside the building a black man was bent over, as a whip lashed red scars across his back. The man holding the whip was Roderick.

Lilias turned and ran blindly, her eyes filling with tears. When she finally stopped, breathless, she was nowhere near her donkey and cart, but on the edge of the open field, near the woods.

As if she never wanted to stop running, as if all she wanted in the world was to put herself as far as possible from what she had seen, she plunged into the woods.

At last she stopped, leaned against a big

boulder, brushed at her eyes. She no longer could hear either the cries of the man being beaten, or the moans of the man in the iron cage.

For a few moments what she had seen was as unbelievable as a nightmare. Roderick, the man who had held her in his arms, who had made love to her, so easily more than once, her lover, Roderick, Roderick . . . everything that had happened between them, every moment they had been together, blurred in her memory, blended with the agony of the man in the cage and the man with the bloody back.

If Roderick kept his threat and went to Ian, if Ian abandoned her, she still would never, never, under any conceivable circumstance, allow Roderick to lay one finger upon her again.

From her reticule she removed the note she had written and with quick angry gestures tore it to tiny shreds and scattered it on the vine-strewn ground.

Now she must find her way back, find the donkey cart, and hurry home.

She looked around, spotted a break in the woods. It must be the way she had come. She ran toward it.

But just as she came close to the open area she knew it was not the way she had come. And as she stood there, hesitant, two men came out of the woods.

She recognized them at once. The two rough men whom she had seen at the springs.

14.

The first one to approach Dragon and Desmond on the hillside above the *Poinciana* was Ned Barnes. Behind him others were shouting and singing; Ned did not appear to be drunk. He walked toward them with firm, definite strides.

He stopped short and looked from one to the other.

"I thought you were leaving the ship tonight," he said to Dragon.

"I changed my mind."

Barnes looked at Desmond. "Your little friend here," he said sarcastically, "ran out on the party."

"He's young. Remember that."

"Oh, yes. I'll remember." Barnes gave her a resentful look. *He doesn't know I'm a girl*, she thought, *not yet. But he hates me. And if he does find out he would be the first to come after me. And the worst.*

She shoved her hands into the pockets where the coins still were rattling. She tossed back her rough yellow hair and looked up at the quartermaster defiantly.

"I didn't want to drink," she told him. "I don't like to get drunk."

The other men were closer now.

"Go back to the ship," Dragon told her.

Barnes laughed. "You need your sleep, little boy."

"Go on," Dragon said again.

"Yes, sir!" She turned and ran down to the beach. A boat was ashore, one of the pirates she scarcely had known before dozing beside the oars.

"Will you take me back, now?" she asked.

"When the boat's full," he told her grumpily. "No need to row out with just you, Monkey."

So it turned out that others crowded in beside her. But she was grateful for the fact that they all were too sodden with drink to pay much attention to her.

The next day seemed like a long one but no one bothered her. Most of the crew felt miserable and went about what duties there were in glum silence.

Dragon and Ned stayed in their cabins.

Desmond helped Bombo with sail mending. He asked, of course, about what had gone on in town the night before. She passed it off, much as she had to Barnes, that she had not wanted to get drunk and so had come home early.

"Good boy," he told her. "Smart boy."

Desmond was silent after that. All she could think of was that moonlit beach and Dragon. She could still quiver with the remembering—

the taste of his mouth, touch of his hands, of the wonder of his being inside of her, the way they had been one. When, oh when, would she be alone with him again?

By the second day the men had finished overhauling the ship and she was ready to sail the next morning. A rumor circulated: there was going to be another attack.

More booty, thought Desmond. But more important, there might be a chance to prove to Dragon once more that she could be useful.

She was leaning on the rail, looking out at the stars shining over the water. The seas were quiet that night and the air was fresh and sweet after a shower. She was again remembering the moonlit night on the beach, and Dragon. How wonderful it had been to be a woman! She sighed.

Someone behind her asked, "What are you doing, Monkey; staring up at the stars?"

She turned around. It was pug-nosed, brawny Romly. He was grinning.

"I was," she told him, and turned her back again.

Romley stood beside her, and gave her a good-natured shove to the side.

"Why'd you run off the other night, Monkey? You missed a lot of fun. You scared of women?"

"No."

"I think you're a virgin."

"No, I'm not." She could not look at him.

"I think you are. I think maybe you're just

too young. Here, let me see what kind of man you are." He reached one hand toward her crotch and she jerked away.

"Come on, now, Monkey . . ."

She ran across the deck and climbed the ladder to the great cabin.

Dragon had promised to keep her secret. Dragon would protect her.

But outside the door to his quarters she stopped because she could hear voices from inside.

"You objected to this ship," Barnes was saying. "But now you can see what it can do, how much better than that little tub we first had. And now you object to a simple, harmless strategy which may bring us a fortune."

"You know why I object."

"I know. Women. Women you want to put on pedestals. The lengths you go to protect that . . ."

Desmond caught her breath. Had Dragon broken his promise and told Barnes about her?

But Dragon interrupted the quartemaster.

"That is none of your affair, Ned. That has nothing to do with our business arrangements or how we handle this ship. We do not take prisoners. We do not capture women."

"She'll come to no harm. Not if that rich husband of hers pays off."

"No."

Silence for a moment. Then Barnes said in an

unusually quiet voice, "But aren't you leaving the ship tonight?"

Again Desmond caught her breath. He mustn't leave! He mustn't!

"You mean, when I am not aboard . . ."

"Then I'm in command. That was our agreement, wasn't it?"

Desmond heard footsteps behind her. She looked back. Sure enough, Romley had followed her.

She began pounding on the door.

Romley came no closer and in a moment the door had been opened.

At first she could think of nothing to say, just stood there feeling helpless. Finally she stammered, "There's trouble below, sir."

Would that make Dragon immediately leave his quarters, leaving her alone with Barnes? To her relief Dragon said quietly, "See to it, Ned," and Barnes rushed past her.

Dragon came over and closed the door behind her.

"What is it, Desmond? What's the matter?"

She had run to him for protection but now she hated to confess why. Yet there was nothing she could do but to tell him.

"One of them tried to touch me."

"He guessed you were a girl."

"Oh, no. No. He didn't guess. He . . ." How to say it? Finally she said simply, "He was trying to find out. He would have. And so I ran."

"And by running to me . . . do you know

what Ned will think? What the others may? Because of the way I have treated you?"

She shook her head.

"Oh, Desmond, Desmond." He put his hand on her shoulder. "Desmond, you are such an innocent. Don't you know that men . . . and boys . . . when they are away from women, when they are off to the wars or out at sea . . . often have relationships with each other?"

"No, I don't know." She didn't even really know what he was talking about. Surely not—.

"So, you see, you are in double danger."

She nodded. She swallowed, trying to digest the meaning of his words.

"And you see why, more than ever, I must get you off this ship, back on land where you belong."

"No, Dragon, I want to stay here. I want to help you." What could she do to convince him?

He put his other hand on her other shoulder and looked down into her eyes.

"And have me worry about you every moment? You've been on my mind almost constantly since the other night."

"You've been on my mind, too!" she cried.

Again, as she had that night on the path down the hill to the bay, she threw her arms around his neck, and again he held her close.

She turned her head so that her face was directly in front of his and it was the most natural thing in the world for his lips to meet hers.

It was a long kiss and when it was finished he still held her in his arms.

"Desmond, oh Desmond, what you do to me!"

He pulled away from her and tossed his head toward the door, in warning.

Already she could hear footsteps. There only was time to move a few feet farther apart before Barnes opened the door and came into the cabin.

"There was no trouble," he said coldly.

He was staring hard at Dragon, his narrow eyes even narrower with curiosity, suspicion.

Dragon spoke as if she were not there.

"This ship is no place for the boy. I'm finding him a spot ashore."

"No!" Desmond was beyond caring now if her secret were out. Let them know she was a girl; let them all know; she loved Dragon.

"Yes." Dragon's voice was stern, the voice of the captain. "I'm going ashore before dawn. I shall make arrangements."

"Are you taking him with you?" Barnes asked.

Desmond's heart jumped.

Now Dragon's face was thoughtful. After a moment he said, "No. Not now. I shall leave him in Bombo's charge. Do you understand, Ned? The boy is to stay close beside Bombo; no one is to annoy him. Until I return."

Barnes shrugged; his smile was sneering amusement.

"Take him to Bombo, and give Bombo his orders. *Now*."

Dragon turned his back on them and Barnes gave her a little shove toward the door.

Desmond was thoroughly frightened now. She determined to stay very close to Bombo. Not that the old man would be much protection, but Dragon had given the order and she was certain it would be obeyed.

She went below and moved her hammock closer to Bombo's, but she only half-slept all that night.

The moon had set, the sky and the sea were black as the unknown.

Just before dawn she was aware of movement aboard, quietly got up and stood by the rail. Dragon was going ashore. She watched him jump out of the small boat and wade the last few feet. In the half light his firm, erect body was silhouettted.

His hair was shorter than most men's; he was neater, more of a piece. He was different from anyone she had known in her whole life. *Oh, Dragon, I love you so!* She sighed with remembered happiness and prayed that it would happen again.

He had disappeared on land; the gig was on its way back.

She must try to sleep.

They did not attack a ship after all, that morning. They stayed at anchor and once more she helped Bombo, this time with the pots in the galley.

It was in the afternoon that Barnes suddenly appeared beside them.

"Where are Freedman and Foxy?" he asked Bombo.

"Don't know." The old man shook his head and looked down at the pot he was cleaning.

"That's what every damn fool has been telling me." Barnes turned on his heel and stormed off.

As soon as he had gone Desmond asked, "Do you know where they are?"

"I think I do." Bombo did not look up.

"Why didn't you tell him?"

"Because it would make him angry and he would take it out on me. Of course he wouldn't really be angry because probably he wants them where they are. But he knows that Dragon would be furious."

"Where are they, Bombo? Can't you tell me?"

"Keep your mouth shut?"

"Of course!"

"They've gone to get that vixen who poisoned our men."

15.

The two men who came out of the woods moved quickly across to where Lilias stood. They wore ragged, greasy clothes, bandannas and floppy hats over the matted hair that covered their scarred faces. Her eyes fell to the long knives at their hips, and she was frozen with fear.

Their lips were smiling, but their eyes were dark with hatred.

She managed to say, "Good afternoon . . ." but they did not answer. They just kept coming closer until one stood on each side of her.

One grabbed her and she screamed but swiftly a hand covered her mouth while the other man tore his sash from around his waist and gagged her. Then her arms were tied behind her back, and the bigger of the two slung her over his shoulder, head down, and holding her by her ankles strode back into the woods from where they had come.

Could Roderick have heard her scream? Even if he had, even if he had known who it was, he could not have caught up with these two.

Hanging there helplessly she could not see where she was going. There was only brush and stones and the pirate's big-booted feet.

The brush and stones soon changed to white sand and she knew they had reached a beach. She was dropped on the sand, then pulled to her feet.

She had lost her bonnet and her hair tumbled about her face as one pulled the cloth from her mouth.

He was grinning. "Go on, scream all you want to, Mrs. Gresham. He can't hear you!"

Lilias' mouth fell open in surprise, as a flood of understanding poured over her. Of course that was who they thought she was! They had seen her that day with Roderick's arm around her.

She said, "But I'm not Mrs. Gresham!"

He only laughed. Then he turned to his companion. "Foxy, signal the boat."

"But, I'm *not* Mrs. Gresham, I tell you! I'm . . ." She broke off. She did not want to tell them who she really was; could not tell them.

"Then who are you?"

"I'm a friend of the Greshams. I was calling on them."

"Calling on them? Alone in the woods?"

"I swear it! I tell you . . ."

"Be quiet or I'll tie your mouth again."

He slapped her across the face.

Lilias cringed away from him and looked about her. She could see at anchor a big red and yellow schooner with the large figurehead, of a black-haired woman. She moved a step away from the man who had slapped her, then started to run up the beach, but she had only taken a few steps before he caught up with her, grabbed her by her tied wrists and flung her down on the sand.

"Don't try that again!" he snarled.

She was no match against the two of them. There was no way she could stop them from taking her aboard that ship.

Slowly she pulled herself up to a sitting position and helplessly watched the approaching gig.

The man called Foxy turned to his companion.

"Careful, now, Freedman. Maybe Dragon's on board."

I hope not. If he is, we'll have to hide her somewhere. The caves, maybe."

The gig was in wading distance now.

Freedman called out, "Dragon aboard?"

The boatman nodded.

"Then go back. Say nothing about us. Understand?"

The boatman nodded again and slowly rowed away.

Freedman dragged her to her feet.

"Come along, lady." The word lady was all contempt. "It's the caves for us."

He pulled her stumbling over the sand, inland, down a rocky part of beach to the entrance to the caves. She was shaking now and the tears were starting to come; but she was too frightened to cry aloud. Inside the black cave he again pushed her down. The ground was rough and wet.

"Don't yell again," he warned her. "Don't try to run away. If you behave yourself you'll be all right. We're not going to hurt a valuable piece of property like you."

"But I'm not Mrs. Gresham! I'm not your precious piece of property! Let me go! Just let me go! I'll not tell anyone about this—this mistake!"

Freedman gave her a long look. "I don't believe you. Now quiet!" He lifted a threatening hand.

Freedman stood guard over her while Foxy waited near the entrance to the cave, watching the bay.

Outside it grew dark; night came on and she dozed, fitfully. Her head was aching now and every bone in her body was weary. Not until dawn was breaking did she finally fall asleep. She opened her eyes to broad daylight to see Foxy raising his hand in a signal, and soon Freedman was dragging her to her feet.

From outside the cave she could again see the gig, just off shore. Freedman grabbed her, threw her over his shoulder again, and waded out into the water. He dropped her into the gig, and swung himself in, followed by Foxy. The boatman gave her a curious glance.

"So this is the one."

"She says she's not but I don't believe her."

The boatman spat over the side.

"All women is liars," was his only comment.

As they came closer she could see the name of the boat, *Poinciana*. A beautiful name and a beautiful ship, but above, along the railing, were a half a dozen men, all staring down at her the way her two captors had, grinning, with hate in their eyes.

She had read about privateers, long ago, in London; read of their cruelty to women. To what lengths might these men go, believing her to be the hated Mrs. Gresham who had poisoned their shipmates! Rape? And then when they were through with her, they would kill her.

Once more she tried. "I'm not Mrs. Gresham, I tell you! I am Mrs. Everett and my husband . . ."

Again Freedman slapped her across the face. From above her there came a roar of laughter.

The sash went over her mouth again and was tied, so firmly that it was painful.

When they reached the side of the ship Foxy started part way up the rope ladder and Freedman lifted her up to him. He carried her to the top of the ladder and dropped her on the deck.

"Here she is, Ned!"

She looked up.

One man was standing in front of the others, the ugliest man she thought she ever had seen. Only one ear, a twisted nose, small hard eyes buried in a scarred face.

"Get up!" he commanded.

She obeyed.

He looked at her with somehow less hate than the others had shown. It was as if he found it hard to believe that this was the sort of woman who would trick anyone with poisoned tea.

"So this is the vixen."

If only that gag were not in her mouth! If only her hands were not tied so she could pull it away and once more blurt out the truth of who she was. Somehow this man, ugly as he was, seemed more of a human being than the two who had brought her here to the ship. She tried her best to plead for freedom with her eyes. She shook her head vigorously.

"Hide her, Freedman," the ugly man said. "In your cabin, but don't lay a hand on her. Lock her up and bring me the key." Then he stepped back a pace and looking around him, raised his voice. "Not a word about this. You understand? Not a word!"

"Aye aye, sir! Aye aye!" they all chorused.

Freedman took her by the arm and pulled her after him, but less roughly than before. This ugly man called Ned was obviously someone of authority. As was the one with the strange name of Dragon.

She was led along the deck, then through a doorway to the interior of the ship. Foxy walked ahead of them and she watched him, in the half-dark, open a door.

The light in the room was from one small porthole, high on the wall.

Freedman pulled the gag from her mouth while Foxy untied her wrists.

"Now you wait," he said brusquely, and pushed her into the cabin. Then the two men walked out, closing the door and locking it behind them.

She first thought of crying out for help. But who would come? Whom could she possibly trust on this ship? She remembered all too well the hatred in all those faces. And even if she were able to convince anyone of them that she was not Mrs. Gresham, she was a woman. And they were pirates.

Not since childhood had she wanted to pray so fervently.

She knelt down and lifted her eyes to that one porthole. But no words came. Then she thought: *There is no hope for me, there is no use in prayer. This is my punishment for my sin. This is God's punishment, so there is no use in asking him to save me.*

After awhile she could feel the ship begin to move, very slowly. There were indistinguishable sounds from outside. She remembered her voyage from England to the new world; how she had lain in her cabin, seasick night after night, thinking she would never never reach the West Indies and Ian.

Now there were voices just outside the door. She got up and went close to the door to listen.

"I'll stand guard." It was Freedman again. "You take the food in, Monkey."

"All right." A young voice.

The door was unlocked and a slender boy with a shock of yellow hair stepped inside. He was carrying a bowl in one hand. He stopped just inside, and the door was closed behind him. His bright black eyes were aglow with curiosity.

His first words were, "Are you hungry?"

"No."

The boy stepped forward, the bowl extended, as if he were afraid of her.

"There won't be anything else to eat for a long time."

So they weren't planning anything yet.

Reluctantly, she took the bowl and sat down on the edge of the bunk. It was some kind of stew of beans and meat and spices. She looked down at it in doubt. No fork? No spoon?

As if the boy guessed her unspoken question he said, "We eat with our fingers on ship." Then he sat down beside her. "I have to wait till you're finished."

Even if she had been hungry, the food was

terrible. She plucked out a piece of meat with her index finger and thumb, and chewed on it for a bit. It was uncomfortable trying to eat with the boy staring at her. Yet he was not looking at her as the others had; his face held only a frightened curiosity. His presence helped to ease her, to give her a sense of hope that not all the buccaneers were ruffians.

She tried smiling at him and he halfway responded.

"What's your name?" Lilias asked.

"Desmond. Desmond Duval. And you're ... Mrs. Gresham."

The way he said it, as if he did not quite believe it, made it easy for her to say, "No, I'm not."

"You're not?" Incredulous but not completely doubting her denial.

"No. But those men wouldn't believe me." She looked at Desmond earnestly.

"You don't look the way I thought Mrs. Gresham would look. You don't look like someone who would poison people!" the boy said.

"Thank you."

"But how did it happen? Why do they think you're the—other lady."

There was no point in not telling the truth, now. If those men had their way she would be fighting for her very life.

"They saw me with Rod . . . with Mr. Gresham. They thought I was his wife." And yet, saying it, remembering how they had seen

211

her, with Roderick's arm around her, she was embarrassed.

"Didn't you tell them who you were?" Desmond asked.

"I tried. But they wouldn't listen. That one man slapped me across the face and gagged me."

"That's awful!"

"Do they really care if I'm not Mrs. Gresham? Isn't it enough that I'm a defenseless woman?"

Desmond gave her a long, perceptive look.

"I guess not," he said slowly. "Except that they hate her. They shouldn't hate you."

"That big ugly man who ordered me down here . . . is he the captain?"

"Who? Oh, you must mean Ned Barnes. No, he's the quartermaster. Dragon is the captain. He's . . . *he's* handsome."

Now it was Lilias' turn to be curious.

"Oh? They're hiding me from him, aren't they?"

The boy nodded.

Here was a thread of hope. Or was it? Hadn't she read that it was always the captain who had first choice of any spoils, material or physical?

"Why are they hiding me, Desmond? Do you know?"

Desmond looked down. "I don't think Dragon likes to take prisoners. He's too good a man."

212

"Good? The captain of a pirate ship? A thief and a murderer?"

"He's not that! Dragon's good. And fair. Everybody says so!"

The loyalty was impressive. Lilias' hope rose again. If Dragon were all the lad said he was, perhaps he would release her.

From outside the door Freedman called out, "Ain't she finished yet, Monkey?"

The boy got to his feet in a hurry.

"Are you finished?" he asked. "You didn't eat much."

"I'm finished."

He bent down and picked up the bowl and turned to leave.

"Desmond," Lilias called after him, and also got to her feet.

He looked back over his shoulder.

"Desmond, will you do something for me?" Lilias asked softly.

He did not answer, just waited, looking shy, and a little suspicious.

Lilias went on. "Will you tell the captain that I am aboard?"

Still he did not answer. He turned toward the door and said, "I'm ready to come out." And in a moment the door was opened and he disappeared and the key was turned in the lock.

What would he do? Would he speak to the captain? She could not be sure. But it had been a relief to tell someone about herself, without being slapped into silence or gagged.

The ship was now at sea, the waves rolling larger and larger.

Bone weary, she lay down on the bunk.

16.

Ian walked slowly up the hills from where he had beached, through the early morning light. It was Saturday and market day and he passed slaves from the various plantations pulling wagons of produce toward Edwardsville. Pumpkins and bananas and mangoes and limes, yellow and green, rinsed to bright hues from a brief shower.

He smiled and nodded as he passed them, raising his hand in greeting. Some smiled back, shyly, unaccustomed to being treated like human beings. Many who knew him, those to whom he had given clothing and medicine, grinned broadly.

Ian hated the very idea of slavery, but he had had to accept it as part of life as he had been obliged to accept a great many other things. He genuinely wished he might treat each of his fellow men as equals as much as it was possible. He liked to help people, which was the only reason he had entered the ministry.

You are a born coward, he often told himself. *You become a coward at the age of three in the*

Great London Fire of 1663. He had seen both his parents die in that fire; it was only a miracle that he was rescued, dragged to safety to a boat on the Thames, unharmed but for minor burns. His parents had been educated people; his father had been a teacher. But Ian did not remember his parents too well; they existed in his memory as a blur of kind faces and gentle hands. He grew up in a laboring man's family. They treated him as they treated their own children, with the customary amount of beatings. They constantly reminded him that he was beholden to them, and that he was not to put on airs because of his parents' higher position on the social scale. He was "that teacher's boy". However, their children treated him as if he really were their brother, for which he was eternally grateful.

As a poor orphan, growing up in the turbulent times of the Restoration, he had had few choices for a career. He was fortunate in his childhood in coming under the influence of a friend of his father's, a teacher-minister who gave him some education, who first introduced him to the writing of John Locke.

But when it was time for him to go out into the world he joined the Royal Navy and became a midshipman. Most boys in his circumstances became soldiers or sailors. The actual sailing, the reading of maps and charts, the whole world of life at the sea, this he had loved. It was as a sailor that he had first seen the West

Indies and fallen in love with them, and determined some day to come back.

The fighting he had abhorred; he hated violence for violence's sake. Most wars seemed utterly pointless, and so he had resigned from the service.

He went back to Chelsea and found himself a room, and went back to see his old friend the minister-teacher. That was when he decided, with his old friend's help, to enter the ministry.

Ian never had "the call." He never looked upon religion in a mystical, fanatical way. Catholicism was much too tightly wrapped up with power and politics, a good show but, to him, a false one. Ian was an ardent admirer of John Locke's belief in the separation of church and state. Protestantism was simply the lesser of two evils. It appealed more to a man's mind than his emotions, the hypocrisy smoothed over with practical applications. The role of minister was closer to that of a doctor, a profession he greatly admired because of its kinship with science. And so, with the old pastor's help, he entered the ministry.

On his way up the hills of Cabra his mind was busy with his next sermon.

It did not matter, of course, what he would say. He was quite aware that his congregation, for the most part, came to church because it was the thing to do. And because it was *something* to do. Church was a place to meet people, an excuse for gathering, for the same reasons that men went to the taverns in the evening and the women went to tea parties. The need to be gregarious was a dominant emotion on a lonely sparsely populated island.

Yet he always tried to find something to say that would be good for them, that would make the rich feel the burden of their wealth, that would give the poor whites—and the few black slaves who were allowed to stand in the rear— something to hope for the future. Many of the poor whites had come to the new world to find a new life and he would like to help them find it. He hated the rich, he pitied the poor, and he wanted to make men equal—if only he could!

As he looked into the faces of the blacks he was passing he tried to think of biblical verses upon which he could base his sermon. Perhaps the Twenty-Third psalm. His congregation was familiar with that one; it would be innocuous and comforting. It spoke with gentleness, and gentleness was needed on this island. "The Lord is my shepherd, I shall not want, he leadeth me in green pastures." He doubted that he could reach those of his congregation for whom the meaning would be most pertinent, the planters had closed minds. Slaves were property, they were not considered as human beings at all. Slaves were to be bought and sold and beaten; the only interest the owners had in the slaves' welfare was to keep them alive and strong for more work. They were kinder to their horses.

The epitome of all planters was Roderick Greshman.

Ian admitted to himself that he did *not* love his fellow men, not all of them. Individuals he could despise, and he despised Gresham, not only for his well-known cruelty but for his hypocrisy. Yet his peers considered him such a charming gentleman! Even Lilias found him charming.

Lilias. What about her?

She would be waiting for him when he got home, smiling her pretty, little-girl smile, telling him she had missed him, making him feel guilty again for having left her alone, guilty for having brought her out here in the Caribbean wilderness, away from her cozy, comfortable, protected life in London—even guilty for having married her.

In his midshipman days he had been a lusty lover with many a wench. Even when he was studying for the ministry he had not been long without one bedmate or another. With Lilias it was a different story.

When he first saw her he thought her the loveliest creature he ever had met. Dainty and delicate, with laughter as soft as the touch of her small white hand. He was overawed by her gentle beauty. She was the unattainable princess from another world. His wooing was half-worship. He could not bring himself to treat her as he had other women. But after they had wed, her fragility cooled his natural passion; it was as if he felt she would break if he were not careful. His lovemaking was a gentle mockery. When he kissed her she did not seem to respond. She accepted his organ as she accepted his kisses, as if sex were something one was *supposed* to accept.

Perhaps it was his fault. He now had the slow reluctant realization that his love for her was not the sort of love a man should have for his wife. He wanted a passionate, lusty love, something he did not believe Lilias could give him.

Still, she was his wife; he wished he might wipe that wistful expression from her soft brown eyes, wished he could make her happy.

So he was glad the dressmaker had come to the island, that he had found the means for her to get new frocks, glad that she now could drive the donkey cart and get about. She did seem happier. And he was glad there was such a person as Jonathan Kincaid here. Jonathan had a quick wit, and was one of the few members of the congregation who really seemed to listen to his sermons, now and then nodding when some phrase pleased him. And Jonathan was good for Lilias; he could talk about the theater, he could talk about London, and in general he seemed to entertain Lilias.

The last person to pass him along the road was not a slave, but a white man. From a distance he recognized old Obediah Jackson, his bald head covered with what passed for a hat, bumping along with a mule cart loaded with kegs of rum.

Obediah pulled to a stop and saluted him.

"Good morning, Reverend. You're up early."

"Just getting back from a trip. You're early, too. I didn't know you delivered your rum overland. It must be a rough journey."

"Sometimes I go overland for a friend. And when I need to go into town for supplies. Besides, my boat has a leak."

"I see. A friend?"

Obediah was a bright, pleasant old man, amusing to talk with.

Obediah grinned. "Madame Collette. The dressmaker. Do you know her?"

Ian nodded. "I should think she would prefer French wine, to rum."

"Madame Collette is a Martinican, I guess you'd say. Not *French* French or I'd have nothing to do with her."

"Of course not."

Obie jerked the donkey's reins. "Good day, Reverend. I know you're anxious to get home."

"I am." Ian touched his hat and moved on.

Obediah was the last person he passed. After that he was alone on the rugged green hillside, his mind jumping ahead to his homecoming.

Perhaps Lilias was not yet awake. Perhaps there would be time to have Zula fill the tub so he could enjoy a hot bath first.

The church came into view, gray, somber, sealed in its weekday solitude. Then the little house, smoke rising from the chimney, the door open.

The first shock came when he passed the donkey shed. The donkey and cart were not there.

Where on earth could Lilias have gone so early in the morning? He ran to the open door of the house.

"Zula Zula!"

She came in from the kitchen.

"Yes, Master?"

"Where is Mrs. Everett?"

She shrugged and shook her head, showing no concern or curiosity.

"You saw her leave?"

She nodded.

"When?" he asked sharply.

"Yesterday."

"Yesterday!" Dear God, what could have happened to her? "Where was she going?"

Again Zula shook her head. Then she turned and went back into the kitchen.

First, as if he still could not believe Lilias was not there, he hurried through the living room and into the bedroom. It was in good order, tidy, untouched, the same as always. Still he looked about, as if she were hiding somewhere, as if there might be some indication of her departure. Had she run away? Had she left a note? But that was ridiculous. Where could she run? No, something had happened to her, and he must find out, at once. No time for a bath or change of clothes. No time.

He ran back through the living room, this time to the kitchen. Zula was in the back entry, bent over a wash tub.

"Zula, are you sure you have no idea where Mrs. Everett was going?"

She only shook her head, as she had before, but now there was an enigmatic expression on the black face which Ian did not seem, in his distress, to notice.

"I've got to go after her."

"Yes, Master." She turned her back to him and bent over the washtub.

Where could she have gone he wondered as he started down the hill. He could not go down to Edwardsville's one street and ask one and all if they had seen his wife. What could have happened to her? An accident with the donkey cart? But where would she go, except to town? Had she taken some lonely ride out into the country? Had some vagabond, some runaway slave attacked her? He felt a moment of pure panic.

He went first to the fort, to report her disappearance to the militia.

The officer on duty received him graciously.

"Reverend Everett, we are honored. What can we do for you this morning?"

"It's my wife," he stammered. "She's . . . missing."

"Indeed?" The officer got out his book and pen. "I'll need all the details you can give me. When? Where last seen? And so on."

"I was off island. I just returned this morning. Our maid tells me that Mrs. Everett left in the donkey cart sometime yesterday and has not returned. The donkey cart is relatively new. She has not driven much."

"I know that donkey cart."

"Has anyone seen it?" Ian cried.

"I've had no report. But I shall send out a search party immediately, covering the whole island. In these days, this is serious, Reverend Everett. Runaway slaves can be dangerous. They have been known to attack lone women. And, of course, there are the pirates. Those scurvy scalawags are capable of anything. But we shall do our best."

"Pirates," Ian echoed, wincing. "I know."

As he left the fort he wondered: where now? Then he thought of Jonathan. Jonathan was a practical man, he might have some information or suggestions.

The sun was higher now and hot on his head. The road was empty; no one was riding or driving or walking at this hour of the day. Even Government House looked deserted when he approached it.

He ran up the steps and through the open door, where the sudden dark of the interior was blinding. Overhead a fan turned in the faint breeze.

Jonathan's door was open, too. Ian hurried to it, hesitated on the threshold. Jonathan was there, bent over his desk.

"Jonathan!"

He looked up. "Ian?" His eyes traveled over Ian's rumpled suit. "What is it?" But even as he asked the question he knew that something was wrong.

"Lilias is . . ." Ian did not know how to say it. Finally he slumped down on a chair. "She's missing."

"Missing?"

"I came home and she wasn't there. She hasn't been home since yesterday."

Jonathan put down his quill pen. "I may be able to help you."

"You know where she is? You know what's happened?" Ian rose from his chair and leaned across the desk.

"Perhaps, but . . ."

"But what? For God's sake, man, tell me!"

Slowly, meticulously, Jonathan lit his pipe. "I know the donkey and the cart were found this morning. On the road to the springs."

"The road to the springs! Why on earth . . ." But his sentence trailed away unfinished because of the look on Jonathan's face.

"One of the men here at Government House recognized the cart. He brought it here, and the donkey. It's tied up in back. In good shape."

"Damn the donkey, damn the cart! Where's Lilias?" Ian was almost shouting in frustration.

"Let's not draw attention," Jonathan suggested, raising a hand. "The governor is in his office today."

Ian rubbed trembling fingers across his forehead.

"Where is Lilias?" he repeated in a lower tone.

Jonathan looked at him steadily, for what seemed a long time. For an irrational instant he felt again the sting of Lilias' slap sear his face. Then he said, very quietly, "I think you had better ask Roderick Gresham."

"Roderick Gresham?" Ian repeated the name, slowly, incredulously. "What are you talking about?"

"It is only a guess, Ian. From having observed Lilias and Gresham together. From the fact that the donkey and cart were found so close to his property. And, from your wife's behavior the last two times I saw her."

The bars of sunlight through the window blind were suddenly dimmed. A passing cloud; that's all it was. But for Ian it had the shock of significance. And yet . . .

"I can't believe it." Ian shook his head. "It's simply not possible."

"Anything is possible between a man and a

woman," Jonathan said, *but not between Lilias and me . . .*

"Not with Lilias." For an eerie moment Jonathan thought Ian was reading his mind.

Then he said, "I guessed something was going to happen between Gresham and her. Long ago I knew he was after her; I knew she was attracted. I should never have suggested the donkey cart. It makes me feel like an accomplice."

For a moment Ian covered his face with his hands. When he took them away his face was pale and distraught.

"Whatever has happened, she is my wife, and I must find her and bring her home."

Jonathan narrowed his eyes. "Forgive and forget?"

"That's not the point. I've simply got to find her."

"Is this our parson speaking?"

Ian got to his feet. "I am also a man."

"What are you going to do?"

"Drive out to the Gresham house. Find out if you are telling the truth."

He walked out of Jonathan's office.

Outside in the glaring sunlight the whole world took on an unreal quality. Was Jonathan right about Lilias? What would he do when he found her? What would he say? He had no idea. All he knew was that he must find her.

As Jonathan had said, Billy and the cart were behind Government House. He stopped to pet the donkey's head and run his hands over the big ears. "Good old Billy, if only you could talk!" Then he unhitched the animal from the post, put him back in harness, and climbed into the cart.

Several people waved to him as he rode down the street, and he waved back absent-mindedly. Of course they were expecting him to stop and chat, as he usually did and they would be puzzled by his behavior, but that couldn't be helped. Everything had changed, everything would be different now, all of his patterned life, if it went on, would be a hypocrisy.

He left town behind him, and started up the road that led to Gresham's and the springs. He slapped the reins against Billy's back, urging him on.

Then ahead of him, around a curve in the road beyond the narrow bridge, he saw a horseman riding toward him. Even from a distance he could recognize the man's massive figure, the flowing black hair, the jaunty broadbrimmed hat.

Ian pulled the donkey to a halt, exactly in the center of the road.

Gresham jerked his horse to a sudden stop on the bridge, stared at the donkey cart and its driver.

There was no hint of guilt in his expression, just sheer amazement.

"Good morning, Reverend!" he called.

"Is it?"

"This is a surprise."

"I'm sure it is."

Now Gresham's eyes were on Ian's disheveled appearance as he asked, "Were you about to pay us a call? So early in the morning?"

"Yes."

"I am on my way to town. Mrs. Gresham is at breakfast, I believe."

"I came to see you. Not Mrs. Gresham."

"Oh?"

"Mr. Gresham, I have reason to believe that you can help me find my wife."

"What?" Gresham seemed genuinely confused.

"My wife has been missing since yesterday. Her donkey and cart were found not far from here."

"How very awkward."

"It is very awkward, as you put it. Have you any idea where my wife could be?"

The smile was unctuous. "My dear man, what a ridiculous question."

"I have one more question—you might also deem it ridiculous. Is it true that you have been seeing my wife?"

As he asked the question Ian began to wonder. What if Jonathan had been imagining something was going on? What if she had come up here for some other reason, perhaps just to see the springs. Had he made a terrible mistake; was he behaving like a fool?

But Gresham, still smiling, said, "Your wife is

a beautiful woman. I won't deny it. I have been seeing her."

"Then where is she?"

"That, dear Reverend, I cannot tell you. I have not seen her nor heard from her, in several days. When I saw the cart from a distance I thought it might be Lilias. So I might ask you, where is she?"

"She was not at home last night."

"And you were?" Gresham asked blandly.

"She was not at home."

Gresham shrugged. "Then all I can say is that she must have found another admirer."

Ian took a deep breath. "You're a liar, Gresham. A liar and a lecher and a hypocrite."

The smile faded on Gresham's face. His eyes narrowed.

"I should hate to strike a man of the cloth. But you are goading me too far. Please move that cart so that I may pass."

"You won't tell me where she is?"

"No. Because I don't know. Perhaps she has left the island. Perhaps she has run away with some adventurer."

"I shall find out," Ian said stolidly.

He began pulling the donkey's lines to one side, to turn the cart around. There was room now for Gresham to pass. Gresham did move his horse forward but stopped alongside the cart.

"You continue to suprise me, Reverend Everett." Now he was smiling again, the familiar, charming, drawing room smile.

"Perhaps I do. Until now you've only known the reverend. Now you have met the man."

"Indeed I have. But the surprise is because you are so critical of me, and of your wife, for a bit of dalliance. What's the bibical line? Let him who is without sin cast the first stone?"

"What do you mean?"

"I only mean that even a clergyman can have his fling. And this is something you can't deny. What I saw the other night along the road. You and that blond wench from the pirate ship who pretends she's a boy."

17.

For a moment Ian was stunned to silence and before he could think of an answer Roderick, laughing, had ridden off.

Of course, Ian thought, *Gresham does not know that that was my ship to which I was taking Desmond. He does not know that I am the one they call Dragon. He knows me only as the Reverend Everett and he thinks that Desmond and the Reverend were having some sort of rendezvous.*

The thought of Desmond made him feel like Dragon again, made him think of the ship and of his life there.

Desmond, the "blond wench" as Gresham had called her—brave and beautiful and wild, like an animal difficult to domesticate.

As Dragon he had not lacked for lusty love but never had there been a woman like Desmond. She had appealed to him even in her boy's role; as a girl she was utterly desirable. From the moment he had touched her breast, covered as it was by a man's shirt, he had known he must have her. Yet somehow the wanting had been tinged with a feeling of evil, of lust. Lust filled with tenderness, he told himself. Pray God that old Bombo was looking after her. She was so much in need of protection. He had had no time to do anything about finding her a place on Cabra. The shock of finding Lilias gone had driven all "Dragon" thoughts out of his mind until this moment.

Where could he take Desmond? How could he find her a home? He scarcely could approach any of his parishioners. Roderick Gresham knew who she was and so would everyone else on the island in no time at all. Desmond was not someone it would be easy to hide. Then he thought of old Obediah Jackson. He had cared for her before. He would take her there as Dragon. To her he was Dragon, and that was the way it would be. He did not yet dare to trust that wild young creature with his dual identity.

But for the first time he began to wonder just how long he could go on being Reverend Everett—and Dragon.

He first acquired the nickname, Dragon, when he was a small boy, living with the Barnes family. Ned, four years older, was the leader of a gang of small boys. Ned made up the rules of the game and all the others obeyed him. Ian, too, obeyed readily. Ned was his best friend. Ned was God in those days, because it had been Ned who dragged the three-year-old Ian out of the burning house and saved his life.

St. George and the Dragon was one of their

games. Nobody ever wanted to be the dragon because the dragon always lost, and everyone had to have a turn at St. George. Until one day when Ned was St. George and Ian was Dragon. Ian broke the rules. He writhed away from St. George's outthrust sword, lunged to the other's knees and floored him so swiftly that the wooden sword was thrown out of his hand.

It was the last time they played that particular game but from that day forward Ian was always called Dragon.

Along about that same time Ned stopped being the leader. No longer did he boss his younger friend around, for he began to respect Dragon's intelligence.

As they grew older they saw less of one another. When Ian joined the navy Ned went out on the streets, and later he became a soldier of fortune. From time to time, however, he would pop into Ian's life—sometimes to ask for money, sometimes just to visit. He heard of the Caribbean from Ian and went to sea on a merchant ship. And, of course, after Ian came to Cabra, Ned turned up again.

On their occasional meetings in their teens Ned had taught Ian fencing. On Cabra, in the lonely months before Ian could save enough money to send for his wife, he saw a lot of Ned. As parson Ian had possession of a small sloop, and he and Ned often went sailing together.

As usual Ned was vague about his occupation, until late one night when he knocked on Ian's door and came in to make a proposition.

His business was piracy.

Ian was shocked, but not really surprised. Already he had become aware of the general lawlessness of life in the islands: every man for himself and the devil take the hindmost. And always Ian had hated the rich and the powerful. He believed in equality not only of people, but of their goods.

As Ned described it, piracy was a respectable business. They were modern day Robin Hoods. Besides, most of their victims were French or Spanish. It was an act of patriotism to steal from the enemy for the sake of England. Not only Robin Hood, but Sir Francis Drake were their heroes. Had not Drake been knighted by the queen?

Ned and some of his buccaneer friends had mutinied and captured a small shallop. What Ned was proposing was that Ian become a partner. They needed him for his seamanship— and for his home. Because from his hilltop Ian, with the help of a spyglass, could see for miles around. From there he could spot ships, and by night he could wave a torch and by means of a code, signal to Ned of ships' locations.

At first Ian refused. But the idea was exciting, and finally Ned convinced him to sign on.

In the beginning Ian was the silent partner, but he became more and more fascinated with the game they were playing, and using the excuse of going off island to visit far-flung parishioners, he could set out in his sloop and join Ned and the crew for a few hours or a few days. None of the crew but Ned knew his true identity. It was not long before his superior intelligence, his expert seamanship transformed him into their leader: Dragon. And until lately Ned had stayed second in command.

Ian never had told Lilias anything about Ned, or their lifelong relationship. The game of piracy was Ian's outlet. As other men drank each night at the taverns, or went wenching among the black girls, Ian sailed with the pirates, found his women in far-flung islands. He planned most of the ship's strategies, directed their organization. They went on signalling by night with torches, and whenever Ian left the ship he would make arrangements for the next time he would join them.

The loot was divided according to the unwritten rules of all buccaneers. Most of Ian's share went, without fanfare, to the poor, especially to the freedmen who were trying to make their way in the out islands, until lately, when he indulged Lilias with the dressmaker.

Now he picked up Billy's reins and turned the cart toward home.

He was due to hear from the *Poinciana* that evening. But this time he could not sail with them, not until he got some word from the fort.

236

His last chance of finding Lilias lay with the militia.

He got home, put Billy and the cart in the shed, and went into the house. Zula was preparing the midday meal.

He did not attempt to explain to her what had happened. No doubt she already knew some of the story, or had guessed, he thought bitterly.

He went into the bedroom to clean up.

There were Lilias' clothes in the wardrobe, when he opened it he could smell her perfume. There were her bottles and brushes on the dressing table. Her ghost was there, the ghost of the woman he had loved, but had not loved enough.

I am to blame for whatever happened to her. Because I loved her as a princess, not as a wife.

He hurried to wash and change, and ran out of the bedroom, slamming the door behind him.

It was teatime when he heard a knock on the door. When he opened it, there was Jonathan on the step.

"I have a message for you from the fort."

Ian's heart lifted. "They've found her?"

Jonathan shook his head. "Not a trace. They think she must have left or been taken from the island."

"I see." Ian's shoulders sagged despondently. Then he straightened. "Come in, Jonathan. Come in. You're just in time for tea."

237

Zula had the tea ready but she did not stay to pour. Ian did so awkwardly.

Jonathan sipped his tea, studying Ian's face. Finally he asked, "Did you see Gresham?"

"I did. He admitted to having been seeing her. But he swore he doesn't know where she is now."

"So he would, whether true or not."

Ian said nothing and, after a spell of silence, Jonathan said, "There's something else I think I should tell you about. Something I did not mention before."

Ian thought: *I don't want to hear anything more. About Lilias. About that devil Gresham.* But all he said was, "Right now I feel like something stronger than tea. But I'd better not. Not in the mood I'm in."

"You're wise," Jonathan told him. "I had dinner one night with Lilias, while you were away. She seemed restless and distraught, and when she asked me to get out the sherry, I felt sure that something was wrong."

"Was that when you began to suspect her?"

"No, that was another time." How much should he tell Ian about himself and Lilias? Not the whole story; the man was hurt enough already. Besides, he might easily implicate himself. "I came to call on Sunday and arrived in the middle of a thunderstorm. She was frightened. She said it was fright, but when she clung to me, I felt . . ."

"Please," Ian interrupted coldly. "Spare me the details."

"No more details, my friend. But there is something else you should know."

Ian sighed. "I'd rather not talk about Lilias any more."

"I'll be brief. First off, she was very nervous that night and she rambled on, inconsequentialities, for a long while.

"It did not occur to me at the time. I suppose because I thought it was all part of her vocal evasion of what was really on her mind. It did not occur to me until later, when her cart was found so close to Gresham's home."

"What did not occur to you?"

"Why she suddenly started talking about the possibility of war. A subject she always assiduously avoided, as you know. She always said, 'let's not talk about it.'"

Ian nodded. "Perhaps more vocal evasion, as you put it?"

"Perhaps. But since the subsequent developments, I've had the notion she was spying."

"Spying? Lilias?" He wondered if Jonathan had lost his mind.

"For Gresham. He is a French sympathizer, you know."

"No, I did not know."

"Oh, Ian, Ian! Think about it. His mother was French. He's English in name only. He frequently has asked *me* leading questions. He pumps Governor Appleby unmercifully."

"What did you tell her?" *I am interested now,* Ian thought. *I'll do the spying.*

"No state secrets. Not to a woman. Just that there is danger from attack from a French ship, the *Fleur de Lis.* But that reinforcements were on the way. What I did not tell her is that reinforcements are slow, but that French barquentine is not."

Ian kept his eyes on his teacup. The *Poinciana* was equal any day to a barquentine.

"Where is this French ship? Do you know?" he asked.

"Our spies on Martinique say it left days ago—no routine training sail to Guadeloupe—our spies on Guadeloupe are not too reliable. So far it hasn't been sighted off Dominica. It's almost due south of Cabra."

"What could Gresham have done with such information?"

"Alert other French vessels. Turn it into a real attack on Cabra."

"I see," Ian said quietly.

"But I did not tell her. So he does not know. Perhaps our little garrison can withstand one ship."

"Perhaps the reinforcements will arrive in time. We can hope." Ian spoke lightly but his mind had become Dragon's again and he longed to rush for his maps and charts to plot the course of the French man-of-war, to figure out the time and place when it would be most vulnerable.

Again he became aware that Jonathan was watching him with those sharp inquisitive eyes of his. *He knows my mind is elsewhere from my words, just as he knew when Lilias rattled on.*

Jonathan said, "You have my sympathy. I realize what you are going through. You're putting up a brave front, but before long the whole island will know what has happened. You realize that, of course."

"I suppose so."

"What will you do if she comes crawling back?"

"That's an ugly way to put it!"

"Will you forgive her her trespasses?"

"Will you please quit quoting the Bible to me!"

Jonathan's eyebrows went up in surprise at Ian's vehemence.

"I'm sorry if I offended you. I've been blunt in the hope of getting you to speak out, not to bottle up all your hurt and disillusionment. It's not healthy. You're so naturally withdrawn, out of the world, that this all must have been a great shock to you. Don't sit and brood. Do something. Anything to take your mind off yourself."

Ian smiled. He almost could have laughed.

"Don't worry, Jonathan," he said quietly. "I shall . . . do something."

No sooner had the door shut on Jonathan, Ian had run to his desk for his Caribbean charts. He had only a sketchy idea of the location of the *Fleur de Lis* but he must plan the best route for the attack. He was Dragon, now. He must start thinking like Dragon.

Later, Zula served him his solitary supper, and immediately after, he dismissed her for the day. The rest of the afternoon was spent with frequent trips to the window with his spyglass. The *Poinciana* was supposed to come within range before dusk, and just at twilight he spotted her on the far side of the island, watched her come in and anchor.

He went outside to wait for the dark to come.

It was a clear and beautiful night. The sky was blanketed with stars, the crickets were chirping and those tropical birds that half sing the whole night long were adding their chorus.

The odor of the sea was wafted even to his hilltop, and he longed to go down to the shore and the ship.

Soon it was dark enough for him to go into the shed and bring out his torch and light it. Then he climbed to the big rock behind the house and held his torch high and swung it in the pattern of his signal.

Within a few moments he could see the light far below, swinging in response.

Again he swung his, spelling out in flashes the words, *I am coming*.

It was a long walk down the hillside, through

the woods, on the road that skirted the town, but he was ready for it.

Jonathan told me to do something. Well, I am.

He laughed aloud.

18.

By the time he reached the *Poinciana* it was quite late. The ship lay quietly at anchor, outlined by ghostly moonlight. He had been unhappy when Ned scuttled the old ship for this prize but now he was glad to have a vessel more capable of attacking the French man-of-war.

He put his fingers in his mouth and his whistle cut sharply through the night's silence to signal the man in charge of the small boats. The boatsman was probably the most stupid member of the crew, which was why he was trusted only with such a simple job, so Ian did not attempt to question him about any ship news.

On board he found members of the crew on deck, some asleep, some holding cups of rum and chatting quietly.

As he made his way toward the cabin which he shared with Ned he glanced about for Desmond, but he did not see her. Tomorrow, before they sailed, he must contrive to get her ashore to Obie. He did not like to think of her being aboard during the attack.

He walked into the cabin without knocking, as usual. Ned was always ready at any time of day or night, to talk of plans of action. Ned lived for action; there was nothing he loved better than a good fight.

To Ian's surprise, when he opened the door, he found Ned sitting alone in the captain's chair, with a bottle in front of him.

"Welcome aboard." His voice was a little blurred.

"Good evening."

There was an odd smug expression on Ned's battered face. "What brought you back so quickly?" he asked.

"Business."

"Business?"

"We've a job to do."

"I see." But the usual alert sparkle was not forthcoming.

Ian sat down opposite Ned, but shook his head when the bottle of rum was offered to him.

He began explaining about the *Fleur de Lis*, where it was, what its route would probably be, where the attack should take place. "Possibly as soon as tomorrow, at dusk."

Ned did not speak, just sat there staring down into his cup of rum.

"Well?" Ian prompted him.

Ned began making little wet circles with his cup on the mahogany table top. "It's risky," he said. "They'll be well armed. Besides, the cargo wouldn't be worth it."

"But it's an enemy ship!"

"I'm more interested in cargo."

Ian looked at him in surprise. Of course he'd realized before this that Ned's motive for piracy was less patriotism than greed. But he had always been ready for a good fight, whatever the odds.

"I've been thinking," the quartermaster went on, "that's it a bit unfair—you spending so much time ashore, me doing most of the work."

"I do my share," Ian reminded him. "I've kept us organized. I've spotted the ships, or found out about ships. I've plotted our course. I've . . ."

He was interrupted. Ned banged his cup down on the table. His voice was rough. "I want more of the booty."

His old friend never had spoken like this before. It was a shock, an annoying shock. It was important that they plan their attack on that ship together. He must somehow placate Ned in order to win back his normal cooperation.

"You'll have your share," he said quietly. "Your fair share."

"But I want . . ." This time the interruption came with a knock on the door.

"Damn, here's trouble," Ned mumbled.

Ian said, "Come in!"

The door opened very slowly and Desmond stood in the entrance. Somewhere she had found a comb to smooth down her shock of yellow hair. Somewhere, too, she had found a fresh shirt, much too large for her. She waited there hesitantly, uncomfortably shy.

"What the devil do you want?" Ned shouted. "You had orders to stay with Bombo. Get!"

Ian's heart softened at the sight of her. He wanted to put his arms around her and assure her that all was well.

He said softly, "What is it, Desmond?"

He could feel Ned's eyes on him; he could guess what nasty thoughts Ned was having.

She glanced at Ned, stepped into the cabin, and then looked directly at Ian. "I have something to tell . . . you." The word *you* was emphasized, definitely a request for him to ask the quartermaster to leave. But he could not, would not do that. Not with Ned in such a belligerent mood.

"Go ahead."

He could see how she was drumming up the courage to continue. Finally she lifted her chin with the gesture of brave defiance he had come to recognize.

"They've got a woman aboard. Locked up."

"No!" He looked at Ned. His old friend was indeed rebelling, breaking all the rules they had set up together. "Is that true, Ned?" he asked, knowing full well that it was.

Ned actually smiled. "It's true."

"But I've given strict orders not to . . ."

"*I* gave the order."

247

"Why? You and the rest have plenty of time ashore for women."

"This is different, Dragon. This is the woman who poisoned some of our men."

Good God. Rowean Gresham here on the *Poinciana!*

"What do you intend to do with her?" he asked quietly.

"Well . . ." still smiling, ". . . I've asked for ransom, first."

"How did you manage that?"

"I sent Kennedy. He's the most respectable looking of the lot. And pretty clever. He delivered my note to the Gresham house and got away. The money is to be brought to the caves before midnight. I warned him there would be armed men at the caves. No foul play or his messenger and his wife are done for."

"And what if the ransom is refused?"

"You know the answer to that."

"Not on my ship!"

"Your ship? It is also my ship."

For the first time in his life Ian saw a new look in his old friend's eyes. A wild, angry hate. The hand that had held the cup of rum now was lifted with a pistol.

"Half the ship is mine. And half of all booty we capture from now on."

"No!"

"Then you're not to fret about what happens to the woman. Ransom is due by midnight tonight."

"I demand that you release her now!"

"You demand nothing," Ned answered through clenched teeth.

He was on his feet now. With his free hand he touched his hip. "I have your gun and your cutlass here. I put them there the moment I heard your signalling whistle. You are unarmed and you will do as I say."

With the gun still pointed at Ian he backed past Desmond toward the still open door.

Ian moved toward him, despite the gun, but before he could reach him, Ned had moved through the door, kicked it shut, and turned the lock.

Ian pounded on the door angrily.

"Ned! Ned! Come back here!"

No response.

He ran across to a porthole and pushed it open, cupped his hands about his mouth and called out, "Bombo! Cruikshank!" and on through name after name. "You down there, this is Dragon! Help!"

No answer from below. The spray blew into his face and after a moment he slammed the porthole shut.

Desmond, who was standing there wide-eyed, cried, "I thought he was your friend!"

"He was my friend, until tonight."

"What if they don't get the ransom?"

"You know, as well as I, what will happen."

"But they mustn't! We've got to save her!"

"I know." But how, he wondered. How to get out of here, how to get hold of a gun.

"Maybe the ransom will come," Desmond said uncertainly.

"That's our first hope."

Again he pounded on the door until it shook. Then he went back to the porthole and called again.

At long last there was an answer—Cruikshank's deep voice.

"Aye, aye, sir!"

"Cruikshank! Has the whole crew mutinied?"

"No sir! Kennedy is with us. And Romley. And others."

"Thank God."

"But they're all in a frenzy, Dragon. About this woman."

"Cruikshank, you must get me out of here so I can take charge. As long as I know some of you are with me, I can do it."

"I'll try, sir."

Then Cruikshank disappeared in the dark.

Dragon closed the porthole.

Desmond came closer to him. She reached up and touched his cheek. "Dragon, I'm scared!"

He put his arm around her slender shoulders. She was slim but not slight; there was strength and warmth in her young body.

"Were you all right while I was gone, Desmond?"

"Oh, yes. Bombo took good care of me. But I missed you. Don't go away again, Dragon!"

"I shan't, for awhile. But you must, tomorrow. Before we go after that French ship."

"Why?" She bristled.

"Because it's not safe for you here."

"But I was with you when you attacked that other ship. I helped."

"I know. But I didn't know, then, about you. I thought you were just a brave boy. Now . . ."

He looked down into her lifted face. There was no need for further words; a kiss told it all.

When he released her, she looked up again, her bright eyes all question. And so he went on. "I'm going to ask Obie to take you in again. You can take the booty you've collected and pay for your room and board, until I can . . . find a proper place for you."

She threw her arms around his neck.

"This is my place," she told him.

He held her close for a moment and then he said, "Desmond, you've got to try to rest. Things will be rough in the morning."

He led her to a bunk and persuaded her to lie down. He sat beside her and watched until she fell asleep.

A long while later the ship's bell tolled midnight. There had been no sound before that, no halloos from shore, no movement of a boat. The ransom could not have come.

When the first creeping hint of dawn was coming through the portholes he awakened Desmond.

There were noises aboard ship, running feet, doors opening and closing.

Dragon again went to a porthole and called out and again pounded on the door.

Now there was noise directly outside the locked door, the sound of scuffling, and then pounding, then a great crash that battered the whole door in.

Framed in the doorway were Bombo and Cruikshank.

"Thank God you finally got here!"

"We would have come sooner." Bombo nodded. "But Freedman had the key. And Foxy was standing guard here all night, with a gun. Most of us have been held at gunpoint. But Cruikshank and me, we broke loose. You'd better hurry, sir. They've got the woman on deck."

Ian brushed past the men in long swift strides out onto the poopdeck.

The sun was coming up over the edge of the horizon, stars and the ghost of a moon still there in the pale blue sky. To the west the clouds were tinted pink, like the memory of a sunset.

On the deck below a dozen men had formed a jagged circle. The woman lay in the center, two men holding her by her arms, her long skirt had been pulled up and covered her head. Her bare white legs were writhing in the gray morning light. There were muffled screams as Ned straddled her.

Ian cried out, "Ned! Stop!"

Ned paid no attention.

A few heads were lifted but most of the men went on watching, eyes shining excitedly, lips drooling, their hands at their trousers, fumbling in anticipation.

"Barnes, this is a command!"

Ned did not move, nor look around.

Ian was grabbed from behind, a firm grip on both his arms. He half-turned his head. It was Freedman and Foxy, holding him. With their rough sinewed hands.

"We all get a turn," they told him, leering.

"Ned, in the name of heaven, stop!"

Freedman slapped Ian across the mouth.

"Be quiet. You're spoiling the fun."

Ned, still kneeling, pulled his trousers back in place. Then he jerked the woman's skirt from her head and struck her across the face and she let out a piercing scream.

Ian struggled to free himself. He hit at Freedman's hand and was rewarded by Foxy kicking him in the groin. He doubled up in pain and then he felt the touch of cold iron and realized they had chained him to the rail.

Another man was on top of the woman. Bardwell's huge body completely covered hers. Her screaming faded, as if she were exhausted, and she was moaning now. Then as Bardwell pulled himself away, Ian could see her terror-ized face.

He could see her face clearly, now the familiar lovely oval face framed in feathery brown hair.

Lilias! Not Rowena Gresham, but Lilias. His Lilias . . .

He cried out through the hand that covered his mouth and muffled his cry. He jerked and strained at the chains. It was futile.

Someone else had a hand over his mouth now, because he could see Freedman and Foxy on the deck below. He had to watch while they took their turns with her.

Suddenly there was new movement on the lower deck. Another voice was crying, "Stop it! Stop it!"

Desmond, one arm raised with a cutlass, was breaking through the rough circle.

Ned, standing next to the motionless body on the deck, gave a laugh.

"You're late, boy; I think she's done for."

Desmond raised the cutlass toward Ned's throat. Before she could strike, Bardwell had grabbed her arms from behind and held her prisoner.

Ned prodded Lilias with the toe of his boot. She did not move.

Desmond broke free from Bardwell. He let her go with a sarcastic laugh.

She climbed up to the poopdeck where Dragon was still chained. Above him was the rigging, which she quickly climbed. Dragon must be freed!

As she had done on that French ship, she

jumped from the rigging onto the back of the man who had his hand over Dragon's mouth.

The hand was removed from Ian's mouth as the man fell. Then he felt the chains tugging. He turned his head. Bombo was unfastening them.

The moment he was free Ian swung himself over the deck rail and dropped to the deck below. The men backed away from him and he ran across the deck, dragged Ned to his feet, and swung him around so they were facing each other.

"I told you, Dragon . . . I warned you . . . If you didn't give me what I wanted," Ned snarled.

Ian clenched his fist and swung. Ned staggered back.

"It's all over, Dragon," Ned said in a rush. "We've had our revenge and we've had our fun. We'll toss Lady Gresham overboard, clean up the ship, and get down to business."

"She's not Mrs. Gresham." It was a voice Ned had never heard from Dragon before.

"What?"

"She's my wife. She's Lilias. And you have killed her."

Ned stared, open-mouthed. In dead silence, the crew moved back, away from the two of them.

Ian struck Ned again, then moved toward him with both fists, pummeling his face and the side of his head, harder and harder, until Ned, his narrow eyes shot with fear, began hitting back.

The sun was up now, the deck flooded with the hot morning light. Ian fought as Ned had taught him to when they were children. Ned was heavier, stronger, more used to fighting, but Ian was filled with such a burning, relentless anger, that fear was impossible.

Ned fought like a cornered animal, his face that of a snarling cat. He knew he was fighting for his life. He threw Ian to the floor, pulled his cutlass from his belt and bent over him, but Ian sprang back to his feet and snatched the cutlass from Ned's hand, seizing the handle with his free hand.

He never had killed a man. He never had wanted to, and he did not want to now, not the man who had been his oldest friend. But Ned had killed his wife, and Ned must die.

He swung the cutlass at Ned's throat.

19.

Desmond drew back and covered her face with her hands as Dragon's cutlass slashed a red line across Ned's throat.

She had witnessed bloodshed before, but this was different and terrible. When she saw what they did to that woman, she realized that might have happened to her on that other ship, and even on this one, had it not been for Dragon. No wonder Dragon had turned into a mad man. His wife! That pretty gentle creature to whom she had brought food.

She took her trembling hands from her face but she still could not bear to look at the two bleeding bodies, or the man standing there with the cutlass in his hand, his face lowered.

She moved quickly between the men to where Bombo was standing.

"Oh, Bombo, wasn't it awful?" She could feel the tears in her eyes.

He put his hand on her shoulder, gently. "It was an ugly sight."

"I don't know what to do. I think I'm going to cry. But I mustn't."

"It's all right . . . lass."

She looked up, startled. "You knew?"

"I'd begun guessing. But just now, the way you run up to me—you're not fooling anybody. Not no more."

Then she heard Dragon's voice, clear and loud.

"Listen to me. All of you."

She turned around. They were listening, all of them.

He stood straight and slim in the center of the crowd.

"I am now the master of this ship. The only master. Do you understand, you mutinous bastards?"

No answer.

"You deserve what just happened to Barnes." The he swung around in the direction of Freeman and Foxy. "You two deserve a keel-hauling. Cruikshank?"

"Aye, aye!"

"Put these two in chains. At once!"

Freedman and Foxy turned as if to run but several other members of the crew blocked their way as Cruikshank seized them with his two brawny arms.

Ian swung his head from one face to another.

"How many of you will swear allegiance?"

Bombo was the first to cry, "Aye, aye, sir!" Desmond also cried, "Aye, aye!" and slowly more "ayes" came. Ian seemed to be counting the voices until he knew there would be enough to form a crew, and then he said,

"Those who do not swear will walk the plank. Understand? Now we can get back to work."

There was a patch of silence. Then Romley, who had moved toward the bodies of Lilias and Barnes, asked, "Overboard with these, sir?"

Dragon turned on him, his face full of anger.

"No! We are not consigning them to the sharks. We're taking them ashore for a decent burial. Get blankets. At once. And prepare to disembark."

He threw the cutlass on the deck and strode away, toward the ladder to the poop deck. He hesitated as he approached Desmond and Bombo, only long enough to tell her, "Get your gear, Desmond. We're going ashore."

An Dragon went by, Bombo looked down at her, questioningly.

She explained, "He wants to leave me there. With old Obie."

Bombo nodded.

"But I don't want to leave the ship! I don't want to leave him!"

"You're in love with Dragon, aren't you?"

"Yes, I am!"

"Then do what he says. Get your things and go!"

For a minute she thought of defying Dragon and hiding herself somewhere on the *Poinciana*, but then she realized Bombo was right. She had to do what Dragon wanted.

She went below to find her bag of loot.

Desmond was in the first boatload to go ashore.

Dragon did not speak to her as they rode across the water. He was in the other end of the boat and he kept his eyes ahead on the land. His face was grave and drawn and tired; his whole body was taut as if it took all his will-power to hold himself together.

Obediah was walking down to meet them. Dragon jumped out into waist-high water, waded in, and ran up the beach to the old man's side. There was a hasty conversation as the small boat reached shallow water and then Dragon turned and called out, "Desmond, come here!"

As she came closer Desmond could see the expression on Obie's face, a curious one, as if this arrival puzzled him. He was staring steadily at Dragon, in a completely different way from his earlier reception of men from the *Poinciana*.

"You remember Desmond," Dragon said, as soon as she had reached his side.

"Yes. I remember."

"I've brought her back to you. This time she can pay for her room and board."

Obediah had only glanced at her. Now his eyes were again focused on Dragon, still curious.

Dragon asked, "You are willing to take her in?"

"Of course."

Dragon turned to Desmond. "You'll be safe, here."

"When will you be back?"

"I can't be sure, when there's a job to do. You know that, Desmond."

She nodded, miserably.

"Take your gear into the house," he said now, and turned back to Obediah. "There's another matter I must speak to you about."

Desmond walked up to the house, knocked on the door, which was cautiously opened by Peg. Peg flung her arms around Desmond and beside her little Charlie danced up and down with excitement. Their enthusiastic welcome was a delight but it was not really satisfying. She declined the offer of food and drink, saying, "Not yet," and hurried back outside.

Most of the crew were ashore now and were walking in a long line up from the beach to a grassy hillside. It had started to rain and the sky was dark but the men moved slowly. Ahead of them, under a tree, were the two blanketed bodies, and nearby several of the pirates were digging—as industriously as if they were getting ready to bury treasure.

"So you're staying, Monkey."

It was Romley—who had been so insistent that she go to town that night to celebrate, who had tried to touch her that night on deck to see "how much of a man" she was.

She told him, "Yes."

He grinned mischievously. "Shipboard life getting a little rough for you?"

"No!" she said indignantly. "Dragon wants me to stay here."

"I see." Now his grin was slyly knowing, and then he laughed.

"Stop that." Cruikshank's black face was serious. "You don't laugh at funerals."

They climbed the rest of the hill in silence.

The silence grew heavier as they stood there in the rain waiting for the men to finish digging. When they lowered the two covered bodies into the ground Desmond shuddered. It seemed only a few minutes ago that the two had been alive. Now they were no longer human beings; they were being shoveled under as if they had never existed.

The men put down their tools and looked at Dragon. The others gathered in a circle, as they had gathered around the woman on the deck, but this time their faces were sober, almost frightened, and one by one the men wearing hats took them off and held them and let the rain wash over their shaggy tangled hair.

Dragon knelt down beside the two graves, put the palms of his hand together and looked up at the gray sky.

"Our father which art in heaven . . ."

His voice was different. There was no harshness in it but it was strong and clear, wiping away the memory of the killing on the deck of the *Poinciana*. Desmond looked at the men's faces, one after another. They were bending their heads, their rough fierceness dissolved. They were dirty, ugly, beaten men, in the presence of an emotion much bigger than themselves.

". . . deliver us from evil . . ."

Desmond only half-listened to the words. She had heard them before in the plantation chapel on Barbados. They had meant nothing then, only rigmarole. The meaning was not clear now either, but she had a feeling that there was, after all, some goodness in the world.

When he finished the prayer Dragon remained for a few moments on his knees, looking down at the two fresh graves. Tears were running down his cheeks, and Desmond longed to rush forward and take him in her arms. But almost immediately he climbed to his feet and straightened his shoulders.

"Back to the ship, men. We've work to do." He started swiftly walking down the hill.

Desmond ran and caught up with him. "Aren't you going to kiss me good-by?"

"Not here. Not now, my dear." He tossed his head in the direction of his crew. "Another place. Another time."

He touched her shoulder gently and walked on.

Hats back on their heads, the men all were following Dragon. They looked like themselves again; their walk was almost the old swagger. Almost.

They walked past Desmond without looking at her, one after another. She felt like an invisible ghost. But she followed, too, down the hill, not stopping until she was near Obediah's house.

She stood there in the rain for a long time, watching the small boats fill and go out to the *Poinciana* and return, for another load. As the last boatload left the shore, Obediah came up beside her.

"Come inside, child. You're soaking wet."

Peg took her in the kitchen and removed the shirt and trousers, dried her hair with a rough towel, and found one of her own tentlike dresses to put on. Back in the living room Obediah was waiting with a cup of rum and lime.

"Now, Desmond, please tell me what happened. All that Reverend Everett told me was that he must bury two bodies."

"What are you talking about?" She looked at him, completely puzzled. "Who is Reverend Everett?"

"The man who brought you here."

"But that's Dragon!"

"Dragon?"

"That's the only name he has."

Obie nodded. "I'm beginning to understand, now."

"*I* don't understand. Why did you call him the Reverend Everett?"

"Because that's who he is, child. He's the pastor of Cabra's one church."

"But he's the captain of the *Poinciana!*"

"Evidently. On the side. I wonder how long this masquerade has been going on." He nodded his head again several times, his lips moving as if he were talking to himself.

Dragon a minister! She couldn't believe it. And yet, the way he had spoken there beside the grave. The way he had spoken to her other times, so gently . . .

"His first name is Ian," Obie was saying. "He is a good man."

"Oh, I know he's good!" *Ian.* She felt his name with her tongue.

"So what happened, on that ship? Who are the people whose bodies he buried here?"

"Ned Barnes, the quartermaster, the one who took me away from here. And Dragon's wife."

"What! She went with him on a pirate ship?"

"Oh, no! They captured her. He didn't even know she was aboard, not even when I told him they had a woman locked up, because no one knew she was his wife."

Stunned, Obie asked, "Why in heaven's name would they capture that sweet little Lilias Everett?"

"Because they thought she was that Mrs. Gresham who poisoned some of their crew."

Obie shook his head in disbelief. "How on earth could they think that?"

"Because she was with that man Gresham."

"Dear God." He shook his head again. Then he asked, "What happened?"

"They asked for ransom but they didn't get it. And they locked Dragon up but he got out and he would have stopped them but two men chained him and he had to see it all."

"See what?"

"What they did to her. What you warned me about. What pirates do to women. And then they killed her—Ned killed her. And so, and so ... Dragon had to kill Ned."

She sighed as she finished and took a long swallow of the rum and lime. Then she said, "It was terrible. I'll never forget the sight as long as I live."

Obediah patted her hand.

"I don't wonder," he said. "But I guess you're through playing pirate now. You're well off that ship."

"I didn't want to leave the ship."

"No? Why?"

"I didn't want to leave Dragon."

Obie looked at her for a long moment. Finally he said, "You're in love with him."

She nodded, remembering that night, remembering every moment of the happiness. It seemed so long ago. She sighed.

"Do you think he'll come back, Obie?"

"We can hope. Look, right now Peg's going to give you something to eat. And then you're going to bed. You're tired and you've had a shock and you've been scared out of your wits. Tomorrow's soon enough to decide what to do with you."

20.

It was quiet aboard the Poinciana; the whole atmosphere was subdued. Ian gave orders for them to sail and proceed easterly along the channel to a small harbor with which they were familiar, to lie in wait for the *Fleur de Lis.* Then he shut himself up in his cabin with his maps.

Whatever love or friendship he had had for Ned had been destroyed that moment on deck when he had seen Ned kneeling over Lilias, yet now he missed Ned, almost in the way a person can miss an aching tooth. Ned had always sat beside him when they planned an attack. Ned had ever been the practical down-to-earth planner. He had been cunning. No other member of the crew could replace Ned. He would have to do it alone.

The rain had stopped. A gentle breeze—not the wind he would have asked for—touched at the sails, and their progress out of the bay was slow.

He got up and went to the porthole and looked back at the distillery and Obediah's little house, and the hill beyond.

Desmond was there. Desmond was safe. The way she had run after him and looked up at him. He had wanted to take her in his arms and kiss her—in front of the whole world. But of course that was impossible. Another place, another time, he had told her. The hour of happiness they had shared seemed a long time ago.

Now his eyes were on the green rain-swept hill.

Ned and Lilias, buried side by side. It seemed unreal, like a bad dream. But he must not think about them, what they had done to him, what he had done to them. This was not the time or the place for philosophizing, for remembering, for conjecture. He must not think about himself, at all, or he would only sink deeper and deeper into a slough of self-contempt.

Watching Obediah's little house recede into the distance he thought: Obediah knows the truth about me, now. Will he be discreet? Obie was a crafty old fellow; he lived on both sides of the law—helping runaway slaves, harboring two himself. It was said that he had fathered a mulatto child, which also was against the law. Ian could not quite see old Obediah going to the governor and telling him Cabra's one preacher was also a pirate.

But, he suddenly realized, *what does it matter if he does? I'm saying good-by to Reverend Everett. I could never go back to that. As a minister I was a hypocrite. Nor was I a success*

*as captain of a pirate ship. I left the ship in
Barnes' charge too much of the time.*

There was only one way to redeem himself,
sick as he was of bloodshed. Despite his wea-
riness, physical and emotional, he knew he
must pull himself together. He must act. Be a
good Dragon. Go after the *Fleur de Lis*, capture it, destroy it, save Cabra from the French.

And then pay a call on Roderick Gresham.

But first, he must punish Freedman and
Foxy.

He had spoken of making men walk the
plank or submit to keelhauling—the cruel
process of dragging men under the keel of the
ship—but now he drew back from the notion of
out-and-out murder to brutality. He would do
what, in the pirates' code, was the merciful
thing. He would maroon them.

On the way to their destination, Deadwood
Bay, they reached an isolated cay.

At gunpoint, screaming protestation, Foxy
and Freedman were put ashore, with a respectable supply of guns, ammunition, cutlasses, and
some dried meat and sea biscuits. They could
fend for themselves while waiting for possible
rescue. They were tough; they would make out.

It was dusk when the *Poinciana* reached
Deadwood Bay.

Ian had had time to bury his emotions
beneath a cloak of practical thought.

He called the men together on the main deck

and by moonlight told them about the *Fleur de Lis* and what they would do just before dawn.

He warned them that this would not be a rich capture. This was a military ship; its greatest treasures would be ammunition and documents.

"This is an enemy ship. We are at war."

Cruikshank said eagerly, "You will let us kill?"

"I will let you kill."

Whenever he had been aboard and in charge he had insisted they only wound. He had taught them to work in groups, some attacking, the others searching for the treasures. He had enjoined Ned to practice the same methods, but now he was sure after what he had seen today that Ned had given them more leeway.

"I will let you kill," he said again," because it is war." Then he began reading off names and telling each one what he should do. Cruikshank and Romley were to be in charge of those fighting on deck; he himself would proceed to the captain's quarters for the documents. Others, with Bombo in charge, would head directly for the *Fleur de Lis*' store of ammunition, carry what they could back to the *Poinciana,* and throw the rest overboard.

"No rum tonight. Have your pistols cleaned and loaded, your cutlasses sharpened. Get a good night's sleep and be ready at dawn."

"Aye, aye, sir."

On the way back to his cabin someone touched his arm.

Old Bombo asked, "Where's Desmond?"

"With Obediah. Didn't you know?"

"I knew. I mean I knew that was what you meant to do. But I didn't know if she'd stay. She was so loathe to go."

"So you know she's a girl."

Bombo nodded. "I guessed."

"How many others . . ."

"Nobody, I don't think. But it's better she's there, sir. She's a brave wench, but a wench all the same."

"I know. Good night, Bombo."

"Goodnight, Dragon. Good luck on the morrow."

"Thank you." He patted the old man's shoulder and hurried away.

It took another day and another night before they caught up with the *Fleur de Lis*.

21.

By the next morning Obediah had formed a plan.

"First off, we must turn you back into a girl."

"What do you mean?"

"I mean we must get you out of shirt and pants and into something that fits you better than one of Peg's dresses.

"How?"

"I have a friend who is a dressmaker. I wish she'd been here when you first came. She could make you clothes. You have money, Everett said."

"Oh, yes! And jewelry, too in my bag."

"And perhaps you could stay with Madame Collette while she is making your clothes. She might even let you help."

"Would she, really?"

"Madame Collette is a good woman. And she's indebted to me. She turned up on my beach here like you did. Well, not exactly; she was rowed in from a boat. Like Peg, she's another runaway slave. From Martinique, which accounts for the French name. She'll probably welcome you just because *you* have a French name. The French are in the minority around here. And not too popular. At any rate, as I said, she is indebted to me. It was I who took her to town and set her up in business."

"I don't want to leave you, Obie. What if . . ."

"If?"

"What if Dragon came back and I wasn't here?"

Obie smiled. "If he comes back, I'll tell him where you are. It's as simple as that."

"I guess so. But would I be safe? There are men in town. Men like . . ."

"Go on."

"Like that Roderick Gresham."

Obie gave her a long look, as if he understood. "Stick close to the madame. I think she's a match, even for Roderick Gresham."

The idea of being a girl again had its appeal. Now she would be able to wear that beautiful necklace of carved gold pieces that had been part of her booty. Perhaps she could get her ears pierced and wear those emerald earrings, too.

By the time they set out for town that afternoon Desmond was begining to get excited about her prospects, albeit she still was apprehensive. It had been over two years since she had been in a town, except for that evening in the tavern.

It was a long drive in the donkey cart, and a rather silent one, as Obie did not have much to

273

say. He was busy guiding the donkey up hill and down dale on what was less a road than a wide, rocky path.

They came to a wooded area, emerged on a hilltop looking straight down a cliff to the channel. Far down below a ship in full sail was careening before the wind. Obie reined in the donkey and they both stared at the ship.

"My eyes aren't so good," Obie said. "Is it your ship?"

Desmond shook her head, disappointedly. "No, it's not the *Poinciana*. It couldn't be."

"Why not?"

"They were going after a French man-of-war. Either last night or early this morning. If they caught it by now they'd be some place dividing up the booty."

She looked down at the bag on the floor of the cart. "If they are successful. If they're the winners," Obie added.

She almost wished she had been aboard the *Poinciana* getting her share of the spoils. But Obediah's two "ifs" made her remember the fighting. And Dragon in the midst of it . . .

"A French ship," Obie said thoughtfully. "Good for Ian." He flipped the reins and they started off again.

The afternoon sun was hot when they reached Edwardsville and he drove more slowly. She began to recognize the buildings she had seen on that evening in town. There was the SIGN OF THE BILLY GOAT. To her surprise Obie stopped the donkey cart in front of it.

"I'm thirsty as a buzzard, after that ride. We need a drink. Besides, when you get yourself in skirts you won't be able to go in such places."

The inside of the stone-walled tavern was dark and cool and near empty. She followed Obie to a bench in a corner.

Just as their eyes became accustomed to the interior dark a voice said, "Good afternoon, Mr. Jackson."

The proprietor? No, it was a man at a nearby table.

Obediah leaned forward, blinking.

"Good afternoon?" he said doubtfully.

"Jonathan Kincaid," the man said. "Don't you remember me? You came to see me at Government House about the work permit for Madame Collette."

The man had stood up. Desmond could see that he was quite young, with a slim, erect figure. A gentleman.

"Of course," Obie said. "I remember you now. It's so blasted dark in here."

"May I join you?" Jonathan already had started across the room.

"Of course."

Jonathan sat down on a bench on the other side of their table, put down his drink in front of him and raised an arm to signal the proprietor. Then he looked at Desmond with sharp, inquisitive blue eyes.

Obie said, "This is Desmond Duval, Mr. Kincaid."

"How do you do."

Desmond managed to nod. She was not at all sure how to behave. She had no idea what to say.

"A stranger in town?" he was asking.

"I'm taking her to Madame Collette."

"Her?"

The proprietor had appeared beside their table and now he, too, was staring at Desmond.

Obediah looked decidedly uncomfortable spoke quickly, the words slurring over each other.

"It's a long story. I'll try to explain. But right now we'd like some rum and lime. My best rum, please."

"Yes, sir." The proprietor backed away.

It was strange after all those months of being so careful not to let anyone know she was a girl that now, looking across the table at Jonathan Kincaid, she was glad that he knew. But perhaps it wasn't strange, after all. He was nice looking. And he was a gentleman.

The drinks were served.

Mr. Kincaid, still looking at Desmond, said, "Mr. Jackson, you did say you would explain."

Obediah cleared his throat. Finally, speaking very slowly, he said, "Desmond is a runaway from a pirate ship."

"I did not run away!" Desmond cried. "I was left. Dragon left me!"

"Dragon?" Kincaid asked.

"Ian. I mean Ian."

22.

"Well, I guess the cat's out of the bag, now." Obediah said.

"Oh, I'm sorry!" Desmond cried. "I forgot it was a secret!"

"It *was* a secret."

"I'd love an explanation," Jonathan told them. "You're talking in riddles."

"Yesterday a pirate ship sailed into my bay. The captain, known as Dragon to his crew, was Reverend Ian Everett." Obie spoke quickly, as if to get it over with.

Jonathan was speechless for a moment. Then he began thinking aloud, putting the pieces together.

"All those trips to the outer islands. He wasn't always seeing parishioners. Sometimes he must have been playing pirate. He had a fine view from his home; he had a strong spyglass. But I always thought Ian was such a gentle soul . . ."

"He is!" Desmond interrupted. "Oh, he is!"

"I think there are two Ians," was Obediah's contribution. "I wonder which is the real one."

Jonathan was still thinking aloud. "He told

me he was a midshipman, once, before he went into the ministery. That would account for the seamanship a pirate captain would have to have. Where is our preacher-pirate right now?"

"In pursuit of a French man-of-war."

Jonathan nodded. "Which is threatening to attack Cabra. I told Ian about it, little thinking . . ."

The proprietor had come back to their table.

"Will there be be anything else for the gentlemen and . . ." He gawked at Desmond again. "And the lady?"

Desmond's face lit up with a smile. A lady. He had called her a lady in spite of the way she was dressed, in spite of her unkept hair.

"I think we'd like another round," Jonathan said. He returned Desmond's smile.

After the drinks were served Obediah was the first to speak.

"I was thinking about Ian, last night, on the way to sleep. Trying to puzzle him out. You know, he lived in a plain little house, he did not even have a donkey and cart until recently. But he was always generous to the poor. That must have been why he became a pirate. He certainly kept it a secret. I don't imagine his little wife knew what he was up to."

Jonathan, his eyes on his drink, asked, "Did you know his wife was missing?"

Obediah and Desmond looked at each other.

Then Obediah said, "Go on, Desmond, you tell him what happened. Who the two people were who were buried on my land yesterday afternoon."

Desmond took a sip of her drink to find the courage to tell the awful story again.

"She was captured by some of the men and brought to the ship. Dragon, I mean Ian, didn't know about it. He wouldn't have allowed it."

"Lilias, Mrs. Everett, was captured?"

"They didn't know she was Ian's wife," Desmond explained. "They thought she was that Mrs. Gresham, who poisoned some of their men."

"It's hard to believe they could make such a mistake, isn't it?" Obediah added. "But, you see, she had been seen with Gresham."

"I see. I quite understand," Jonathan said hurriedly. "But go on, what happened on the ship?"

Desmond, suddenly shy, turned her head as she spoke.

"You know what pirates do to a woman. Most of the men . . . had her. Two men kept Dragon prisoner. And then Barnes, the quartermaster, he killed her. And so when Ian got free he jumped down with his cutlass and killed Barnes. And Barnes had been his friend."

She put her hands over her face for a moment, trying to shut out the memory.

"And you were there and saw it all." Jonathan's voice was soft.

Desmond brushed the tears from her eyes and took another swallow of rum and lime.

The man's curious sharp blue eyes were on her.

"Tell me about yourself. How you happened to be there."

"I was part of the crew."

"The crew!"

"For several years," Obediah explained," she has been pretending to be a boy. But that's all over. She's not going to pretend any longer, are you, Desmond?"

"It's too hard now. I can't fool people any more. Besides, I want to be a girl."

"Where are you from, Miss Duval, isn't it?"

She nodded. "Barbados."

"You're a long way from home. You ran away, I suppose?"

Desmond was thinking: now is the time to start my big pretense. Not to tell anyone, ever again, about who my mother was or why I ran away.

But Obediah was speaking for her.

"She had the childish notion that the only way to get on in what she calls a man's world was to pretend to be a boy. Unfortunately she was picked up by pirates. Twice. Praise be both times she escaped unharmed. And now we will turn her into a girl again."

"I think she's a girl now." Again the young man was staring at her. She was getting a little lightheaded after the second serving of rum. She wondered if she was blushing.

Jonathan went on. "So you're taking her to

Madame Collette. Do you think that's a good idea?"

"Madame Collette is wise. And clever. And she is making her way in the world."

"Not just as a dressmaker."

"I know!" Obediah snapped.

What were they talking about? Desmond felt foggy from the rum.

Obediah put his hand on her shoulder.

"I think we better get you over there now. Come on, young lady!"

"Everybody's calling me a lady today," she murmured, as if talking to herself. "It's nice."

The young man was standing, too. He took her hand and kissed it.

"I hope to see you again, Miss Duval."

"Come on!" said Obediah.

When Obediah reined in his donkey beside the swinging sign with a picture of a paniered lady, the door to the little house was standing open.

Carrying her bag, Desmond followed the old man out of the sunny street into the dark interior.

Madame Collette, busy sewing amidst bolts of many colored goods, looked up.

"*Bon jour*, Monsieur Jackson. This is a surprise!"

Desmond was surprised by the seamstress. She had expected a very black person and this woman was a lovely dark gold color with warm eyes and long, graceful hands.

"No rum today, Collette. I've brought you something else."

"Oh?" she looked from Obediah to Desmond. "And what can I do for you gentlemen?"

Obediah grinned. "Take another look, Collette."

Desmond knew she was blushing now.

The seamstress pushed aside the material on which she had been working, stood up and crossed to where Desmond stood. She looked the girl over from head to toe, her eyes wide with curiosity.

"You mean?" she finally said to Obediah.

"A young lady badly in need of refurbishing. This is Miss Desmond Duval, Collette, a refugee from piracy."

Collette nodded.

"It would be a great favor to me if you took her in. She has money to pay for the clothes you could make for her, she can pay for food, she could help you with your work. That is, if you can find the room here in this little house."

Collette looked skeptical. "It is indeed a challenge, my friend."

"But you will take her in? For me?"

Her eyes were warm when she turned to look at him. "For you, yes."

"Good. I'll leave you two to get acquainted." He kissed Desmond on the forehead and gave her a little pat. "Be good. Do what Collette tells you to do."

"Obie, if Dragon comes . . ."

"Don't worry, child. *If* he comes."

Desmond watched him go, reluctantly. She stood in the doorway as he climbed into the little cart, waved good-by, and was gone. She felt abandoned.

As she turned around the seamstress asked, "And who is Dragon?"

She was in this woman's hands, for better or worse, for the present. She would be honest.

"Dragon," she answered, "is the man I love."

"I see."

"Aren't you going to ask me a lot of other questions?"

Collette shook her head. "Not until you have had a bath and are dressed in something besides those rags." She gave a little shudder. "Come with me."

The next room, curtained off from the front, was the dressing room.

"Wait here," Collette commanded.

Desmond obeyed. She stood there, still clutching her precious bag, and looked about her. Clothes hung from hooks in the walls. There were a few pieces of furniture, including a cot. Across the room there was someone standing, holding a bag. A moment later she realized she was looking into a mirror, one of the biggest mirrors she ever had seen. And there she was, looking wretched. She understood, now, Collette's attitude. She turned her back on her reflection.

A black servant girl came in with a tub and began filling it with water, coming in and out of the room with a big pitcher. Then Madame Collette reappeared with a robe and a towel in her hand, which she dropped on the cot, and a bar of soap that she handed to Desmond.

"When you are thoroughly clean, call to me. I'll be out front."

After the servant had filled the tub and disappeared Desmond put down her bag, slipped out of shirt and trousers and, soap in hand, got into the tub.

It was soft, warm rain water. The bar of soap was perfumed. This was the first real bath she had in years, not since she left the Forrester house on Barbados.

She soaped her yellow hair and ducked her head in the water, over and over. She scrubbed at her neck and her ears, her armpits, her toes. She dug her fingernails into the soap to get at the grime underneath them.

And then she just lay in the tub, soaking, until her fingers began to feel crinkly.

As she stepped out of the tub and reached for the towel she saw that the water was filthy.

She was drying herself when she again spotted the mirror. This time she moved close to it. Again, for the first time since she left the Forresters, she could see her own reflection. She was surprised because the last time she had confronted a mirror she had been a child.

She dropped the towel and stared at the woman in the mirror.

It was the breasts that made the difference. She put her hands over them, and thought of Dragon, and at her touch they stiffened. She half-turned and looked at the reflection of her buttocks and again thought of Dragon. *Oh, Dragon, Dragon, come back to me!*

And then she saw Collette in the doorway, watching.

Embarrassed, Desmond stammered, "I haven't seen a mirror for a long time. It's such a beautiful mirror."

Collette smiled at her for the first time, and said, "It's quite new. A recent gift from an admirer. It came all the way from Barbados."

"So did I!"

"Really? Put down your hands, child, and let me look at you."

Desmond took her hands from her breasts and found herself doubling her hands into fists.

"Turn around."

Desmond obeyed.

"Now turn around again."

At last Collette said, "You have a fine body. It will be a pleasure to dress you."

Desmond grabbed the robe from the cot and hastily wrapped it around herself. It was ruffled yellow silk and swelled of a musky perfume.

"Yellow is your color," Collette said. "We must remember that. Come with me."

Desmond followed her though a small living room, past a door open to the kitchen, and into the bedroom. Collette motioned for her to sit down at a dressing table, then picked up a brush and began to work on Desmond's hair.

"It must grow. It must grow much more. But the brushing did help. See?"

Desmond looked into the dressing table mirror. Oh, Collette had made her hair look so much better!

"You are very unusual." Collette was looking into the mirror, too. "Such black, black eyes. Such fair hair."

"My mother told me that I have my grandmother's eyes."

"Oh? Your grandmother must have been a beautiful woman. My grandmother was a mulatto. My mother a quadroon. I am an octoroon."

She put the brush down on the dressing table but went on looking into the mirror. Her frankness made Desmond warm to the woman.

"My grandmother was a Carib," She said finally. "My mother is a white slave."

"Your Father is French? Your name . . ."

"He was French."

"You speak French?"

Desmond shook her head. "I never knew my father."

"I see. Nor did I know mine."

They smiled at their reflections in the mirror. They were friends.

Collette said, "Let us go into the sitting room and have a drop of rum while Polly fixes our supper."

The room was simply furnished with a few rough pieces of island-made furniture. One shuttered window opened onto the wall of the general store next door. The rum drinks were more elaborate than the rum and lime juice she had had at the tavern. The rum was smothered in many fruit juices and served in large mugs.

Collette asked, "Were you captured by pirates?"

"Not the first time."

"Would you like to tell me about it, from the very beginning?"

Desmond said, very slowly, sipping her drink, "When I got my booty—all that I have in my bag—I planned to go far off to someplace where no one knew me, and to tell no one about myself. But now . . ."

"Now?"

"I'd like to tell someone about it. I'd like to tell you."

Collette smiled. "Thank you for trusting me. I shall tell no one."

So Desmond started at the very beginning, with her childhood and Alan's raping her, and how she had run away and pretended to be a boy; of the *Lady May*, and Batham. Of meeting Obediah, and the coming of the *Poinciana*.

Up until now her revelations had all been personal but when it came to the story of the capture of Mrs. Everett, the rapes, the murder, she hesitated.

"It got too hard to hide the fact that I was a girl. I saw terrible things aboard the *Poinciana*. And when it was decided that I should be left with Obie, I finally agreed it was the only thing to do. Besides, I wanted to be a girl again."

She fell silent, sipping her drink, feeling drained from the long talk.

For a few moments Collette did not speak.

"I have a few questions, Desmond," she said at last. "I know you are not a virgin, because of that rape. But since then, have you ever been with a man?"

Desmond nodded, swallowed. "Yes—Dragon."

"Dragon, the man you love. Who is he?"

"He's the captain of the *Poinciana*. And now they're off to try to capture a French man-of-war. And I . . ." The tears came into her eyes. "I wonder if I'll ever see him again!"

23.

Ian woke before Dawn. It was raining lightly and a wind had risen. The ship rocked gently, the canvas crackling.

He got up and fastened two pistols to his belt in addition to his cutlass. Ned's pistols. Ned's cutlass. A murderer's weapons. But he mustn't think about that, now.

The ship was ready just as dawn slipped over the horizon. The wind was with them, as he had prayed it would be. The *Poinciana* sped out of Deadwood Harbor, along the channel toward the next indentation in the shore line.

Inch by inch, foot by foot, wave by wave, the *Poinciana* moved closer to the *Fleur de Lis*, like a dog following a scent. The barquentine was still at anchor, its stern was toward them.

Silently the *Poinciana*'s sails were furled. One by one the boats were lowered and boarded. The men on deck manning the cannon waited until Dragon, from the first boat, gave the signal.

A broadside winged the barquentine's rigging, sending it out of control.

Swiftly the *Poinciana*'s crew, cutlasses held

clenched in their teeth, climbed the ladders they had flung across the *Fleur de Lis'* sides, cut their way through the nets that were put there to prevent just such a boarding, and swarmed over the quarterdeck.

Romley and Cruikshank led the attack. As Ian came up the ladder he could hear the first screams from the nightwatch.

He scrambled through the fighting men to the ladder leading to the poop deck. Just as he reached the top a door opened and two ship's officers, pistols in hand, emerged, looking groggy and rumpled from sleep. Ian fired twice, shooting the guns from their hands.

"Get below!" he told them, still pointing his smoking pistol in their direction, and they obeyed.

Inside the cabin he shoved his pistols back inside his belt and began searching for documents, stuffing all the papers in sight inside his shirt front.

He was just finishing when a Frenchman appeared in the doorway, gun in hand. He fired, but Ian ducked behind a huge desk, pulled his pistol from his belt, lifted it and fired back. The man screamed as he fell.

Ian stood up, caught one glimpse of the agony on the dying man's face as he stepped over him, and left the cabin.

The sun was up now, shining relentlessly on the turmoil of the deck. Men lay wounded or dying or dead, some of the *Fleur de Lis* crew,

291

some of his own men. He did not stop but hurried below to the cargo area. He had to step aside as some of his men came by, arms loaded with ammunition.

"Is there more?" he asked.

"Lots more. We can't take it all."

"I'm going to find the captain. If he won't surrender we'll put a torch to the hold. Pass the word along."

Ian ran back down to the deck.

"Where's the captain of this ship?"

"I've got him here, Dragon." Cruikshank was standing beside a bound figure. "Saved him for you."

"Untie him."

"What!"

"I said, untie him."

Cruikshank obeyed but he stood close beside him. The captain was a plump young man with a garish mustache and very bright black eyes.

"I'm asking you to surrender," Ian said. The captain did not answer, so Ian repeated it in French. *"Mettre bas les armes!"*

"Non!" the man cried. *"Jamais! C'est impossible!"*

"Then we shall blow up your ship." Again, he repeated it in French. This time the captain did not answer. But he lifted his chin defiantly.

"Abandon ship. Everyone," Ian commanded. "Take the wounded. Take all wounded. You, Bardwell, you, Kennedy, search the ship. And quickly."

Ian kept his eye on the French captain while his men scurried about, carrying the wounded across to the ladders and on to the *Poinciana*. It seemed to take a long while, and all the time the French captain stood there, his chin up, in stubborn silence. He was a brave man. It was a pity that the fortunes of war had made him an enemy.

At last Bardwell came to report, "Ship's clear, Dragon."

"Go back to the *Poinciana*. All of you."

They began moving until only Bardwell, the French captain, and Ian were there.

"What about him?" Bardwell asked.

Ian motioned at the captain but still he did not move. He was unarmed, so Ian left him there under Bardwell's watch on the deck and went below.

He found a torch, lighted in a dark passage way, he carried it down below, tossed it into the ammunition hold, then ran back and up to where the captain stood by Bardwell.

"I've lit the hold. Hurry!

He climbed over the rail. "Hurry!" he called back. Bardwell followed him over the side of the ship into the small boat.

He and Bardwell each grabbed an oar and rowed with long, sure, steady strokes, moving the boat as swiftly as was humanly possible toward the *Poinciana*.

Just as they reached her Ian still could see

the proud French captain on the deck, a brave man, waiting to go down with his ship.

The explosion blasted into the blue morning sky.

"Full sail ahead!" Ian cried out as he climbed aboard.

Slowly, oh so slowly, the *Poinciana* began moving away. It rocked on the violent waves from the explosion, the decks shaking. Then its sails caught the wind and it careened away to safety.

"Edwardsville," Ian told the man at the wheel.

"What?"

"Edwardsville. The harbor. The main dock. We'll turn our prisoners over to the governor. The prisoners and the documents I took from the *Fleur de Lis*."

Already the ship surgeon was tending to the wounded and passing out tots of rum.

Ian went to his cabin and took out the papers he had stuffed inside his shirt and spread them out on his desk.

Not only were there instructions for the *Fleur de Lis* but there was a definite indication that a sister ship, the *Plume d'Or*, was also on its way. His work was not finished.

He copied down all that concerned the *Plume d'Or*, then arranged all the papers in a neat packet.

When he came out on deck the ship was

294

sailing quietly through the morning sunshine along the channel and the whole West Indian world was beautiful as it had been the first time he saw it.

It was good to catch the first sight of the fort with the British flag making a spot of color against the blue sky. He hurried to order their skull and crossbones flag pulled down and the white flag of truce raised in its place.

He stood at the prow of the ship, a sword instead of a cutlass at his waist, lifting his hand in a salute to each of the other ships in the harbor. They saluted back and crowds gathered on the deck of each to watch the *Poinciana* come in.

To his surprise the dock was crowded with people, and as they came closer he recognized Governor Appleby. The crowd set up a "Hurrah!" as the *Poinciana* docked.

Ian went back to the cabin and picked up the *Fleur de Lis papers*. All the way back on deck, and all the way down the ladder, he was trying to think of exactly what to say when he was face to face with the governor.

When his feet touched the dock he walked straight across to Appleby, looking directly at him and at no one else.

The governor was the first to speak.

"Congratualtions, Reverend Everett."

But he was not smiling. Well, Ian thought, at least the pretense is over. He held out the bundle of papers.

"These are from the *Fleur de Lis*. We have the surviving prisoners aboard. We sank the *Fleur de Lis*."

The governor nodded as he took the papers. "We knew. We have had a lookout on Mount Cuerno."

Ian's eyebrows went up with surprise but he refrained from questioning. He said, "There is another French man-of-war on the way. We must go after it, as quickly as possible. But I shall need arms, ammunition, men."

"Of course."

"Thank you. But first, while the ship is being refurbished, I have some personal business to attend to. For that I must borrow a horse."

Governor Appleby nodded. His narrow eyes were curious, now. But he turned toward the crowd.

"The reverend . . ." then he hesitated and looked back to Ian.

"You'd better call me Mr. Everett from now on."

Again the governor nodded, soberly; again he turned.

"A horse, please, for this gentleman?"

Once more he was riding on the road out to the springs, not bounding along in the donkey cart, but galloping on a fine brown mare.

No longer was he the reverend, going to call on a parishioner. No longer was he planning and choosing the gentle comforting words he would have to say.

He rode across the small bridge where he had encountered Gresham before, and straight on to the Gresham plantation, not reining his horse until he was at the foot of the long stone staircase. He dismounted, strode up to the front door and banged the knocker.

When a servant opened the door and stared at him wide-eyed he said, "Tell your master I want to see him at once. Alone. Outside."

As the black girl turned away Ian went back down the steps and waited at the foot.

Quite some moments passed before Roderick appeared in the open doorway.

He, too, was wearing a sword.

He came down the broad stone steps in his usual arrogant stride, stopped on the bottom one so that he was standing more than his usual head taller, looking down.

Ian, his hand on his sword, said, "You did not send the ransom."

"Of course I did not send the ransom. It was not my wife who was being held."

"Do you know what happened?"

"I can guess. That gang of ruffians had a jolly good time sharing the lovely Lilias."

Ian reached up and slapped him across the face.

As Roderick drew back in surprise, Ian went on. "I'll tell you what happened. She was raped and then she was murdered. She died. Because of you. And now you will defend yourself, like a man. If you are a man."

297

He drew his sword.

It had been years since he had fenced. Ned had taught him, long ago, Ned's own peculiar ruffian ungentlemanly fashion, and Ian had been quick to learn. His slenderness, his agility made him a natural fencer. It came back to him now, as his fingers gripped the rapier's hilt.

Roderick had drawn his sword with equal haste and backed up several of the stone steps.

Ian followed and for awhile it was like a mad circling dance, up and down the stone stairs.

A pale fear suffused Gresham's face. His black eyes were not as angry as they were frightened, but he managed most of the time to stay above Ian on the steps, and his strong muscular arms thrust out his sword with a power which, time after time, Ian parried.

Until he caught his foot on a rough spot of one step and felt himself falling backward, Roderick after him, until he was at the bottom of the stairs, on his back.

Roderick lept toward him but before he reached him Ian had scrambled to his feet and drove his sword straight up into Roderick's breast.

As Ian stepped back, slowly pulling his sword free, he heard a scream from the top of the stairs.

Rowena Gresham had been watching.

She was standing there, her hands covering her face. Beside her were servants and the two children.

Ian turned his face away. He pulled his handkerchief from his pocket, wiped the blood from his sword, and put it away. When he looked up in the other direction he could see another audience that had gathered from the slave quarters.

Witnesses, he thought, to a fair duel.

The ride back to town was slow and solemn.

24.

When Desmond cried out, "I wonder if I'll ever see him again!" Collette gave her a long, calm smile.

"If he does not come back, there will always be another man."

"But I love *him!*"

"Despite all that has happened to you," Collette went on, "you are incredibly innocent. Love! It's a moment in the sun; it does not last. You seize upon it as you would pluck a beautiful flower to enjoy, knowing it will not, cannot, last. Perhaps you have lost this love, but it will come again, or you will find another."

"No!"

"Did he ask you to marry him?"

Desmond shook her head. "My mother told me nobody ever would."

"Because of your grandmother?"

"Yes."

"Nonsense. I have hopes for you, child."

"Hopes?"

"Of finding you a husband. I think it can be done. If we hide the truth about your birth, and all that has happened to you."

"But all I want is Dragon!"

"All you want, all you are ready for, is a man. Come, let me measure you and the first thing in the morning I shall get the material for your first dress."

The dinner that evening was not as sumptuous as when she had dined with Dragon on the food from the French ship they had captured, but it was a good meal. Collette had trained Polly well. The sauces were delicate, the meat tender. And there was fresh fruit for dessert.

By the time they had finished Desmond was nodding over banana and papaya, hardly listening to what Collette was saying, scarcely answering Collette's questions. Soon after she fell sound asleep on the cot in the dressing room.

She slept late the next morning and awakened only when Polly tiptoed in with a cup of coffee and a sweet roll.

Polly's eyes were wide with curiosity as she put the breakfast down on a chair beside the cot.

"You slept long time. The sun has been up for hours."

"Madame Collette is already up?"

"Yes, ma'am. She gone to market.

"I see."

"She be back soon. You want more coffee, holler, please?"

"Thank you."

Polly backed away, still staring at her, and disappeared through the door.

Desmond had just finished breakfast when Collette appeared, a large market basket on her arm.

"*Bon jour, petite, bon jour!* And how are you this morning?"

"I am rested, thank you. I slept very well."

"Good, good! Now wait until I take this to the kitchen so Polly can get to work. I have much, much to tell you!"

Desmond could hear Collette jabbering away to Polly in the kitchen. She was there quite awhile, while Desmond found the chamber pot and the wash basin and made her toilet, then slipped into the ruffled yellow robe. She was sitting on the cot, still not thoroughly awake, when Collette came back.

Colletet sat down on a chair opposite her.

"I always do the marketing. I cannot trust Polly to choose the freshest, the best, of vegetables, of fruit, of fish, of meat. Besides, it is at the market where one gets the news of the day. And today there is news." Her eyse were sparkling with excitement. "The pirate ship—what is its name? The *Poinciana*. She has returned, triumphant. She captured, she sank the French man-of-war!"

Desmond's face lit up. She clasped her hands together. "He's back! He's back! Oh, if I only had clothes, I could run down and meet him.

My shirt and pantaloons . . ." She looked about. "Where are they?"

"Wait, wait! You must not be foolish. Besides, it is no use to run down to the dock. The ship is preparing to sail again."

"No!"

"War is war, my child. There is another French ship to be captured."

Desmond's shoulders slumped with disappointment.

"There is other news, "Collette said. "Your Dragon, your captain, is also our Reverend Everett. That is what the town is buzzing about."

"I knew that," Desmond said quietly.

"You knew that? And you knew that he is married?"

"He was married. But his wife is dead."

"Dead? Why only the other day she was here. I have a dress ready for her." She pointed to one of the garments hanging on the wall of the dressing room. "Dead? I can't believe it!"

"Murdered," Desmond said. "I saw it happen. The pirates captured her. Dragon, I mean Ian, did not know about it. They held him prisoner and he saw it happen."

"How dreadful!"

Desmond sighed. "I don't want to talk about it. I don't want to even think about it, ever again!"

Collette crossed the room and put her arm across Desmond's shoulders.

"Come out in the shop. Let me show you the material I found for your frock."

Desmond spent most of the day watching Collette cut and pin together the yellow cotton goods. The door to the shop was kept closed that day, and when there was a knock on the door Desmond would flee to the dressing room.

Late in the afternoon, after she had run into the dressing room, Desmond recognized the voice of the young man she had met in the Sign of the Billy Goat.

"Why, Monsieur Kincaid," Collette said, "to what do I owe the honor of this visit?"

"I bring you news. The latest vews of the day."

"The *Poinciana* did not sail?"

Impulsively Desmond pushed the curtain in the doorway aside, just as Jonathan was saying, "The *Poinciana* did sail, but before she sailed . . ." He broke off and stared at the girl in the doorway.

Collette said, "This is Miss Duval."

"We met. Yesterday. Good afternoon, Miss Duval."

"Good . . . good afternoon," she stammered. "What is the news?"

"There was a duel, before the *Poinciana* sailed. A duel between Ian and Roderick Gresham."

He was looking at her so seriously that Desmond shook with apprehension.

"Gresham is dead," he said at last.

She sighed with relief.

There was another knock on the door.

Collette, her eyes twinkling, said, "I really think, Desmond, you should stay in the other room."

Later, when they were in the sitting room enjoying their rum drinks, Desmond asked, "Who is that Jonathan Kincaid?"

"A very pleasant young man, isn't he? He works in the Government House. Sometimes he drops in, just to chat. I think he is lonesome."

"He is very good-looking."

"Yes, he is. And he is a bachelor. Therefore, a possibility," Collette said slyly.

"Possibility?"

"For a husband."

"Oh, no!"

"At any rate, be nice to him. In case your pirate-preacher never comes back."

Two days passed.

The yellow dress was finished. Collette had also made her a shift.

Desmond put them on in the dressing room, in front of that mirror. It was a simple cotton frock, with modest paniers. But its fit kept it from being plain. It followed the curve of her bosom, and for all its simplicity it was provocative. A pair of Collette's shoes, the toes stuffed with cotton, were on her feet.

Polly stood in the doorway, admiring

Collette said, "Now you are ready to face the world."

Now that she had a dress she could sit in the front room, and the door could stand open. She could watch passersby, she could be introduced to wide-eyed ladies who came to the dressmaker's.

She helped Collette lay and cut out another dress for her, a white silk organza. She was learning about dressmaking. It was all very new and exciting and she was almost happy. Except when she thought of Dragon.

She was there in the front room the afternoon Jonathan Kincaid again came to call.

"Miss Duval, how charming you look!"

"Thank you. Collette did it."

"Madame Collette had good material to work with."

"You like this yellow cotton?"

"I wasn't referring to that material. I was referring to you."

"Oh. Thank you!" Desmond felt herself blush.

After a moment Collette asked. "And what is your news today, Monsieur Kincaid?"

"No news, today."

"No word from the *Poinciana?*"

"No." He cleared his throat. "I came today to ask your permission to take Miss Duval for a ride."

Collette laughed. "This is a new role for me, being a duenna. Of course you have my permission."

Alone beside the young man in his two-seater carriage, Desmond was not sure of what to say or how to behave. Jonathan, at first, had little to say himself, and kept his eyes on the road.

They drove out of town past the entrance to Gresham's plantation and the road that led to the springs, along a palm-shaded lonely road from which she could look down between the trees to the blue water and the dots of green islands in the distance.

At the top of a hill he reined the donkey to a stop.

"Beautiful, isn't it?" He turned and looked at her for the first time.

"Yes, it is," she answered, unable to think of anything else to say.

"May I call you Desmond, Miss Duval?"

"If you like."

"Are you enjoying it with Madame Collette?"

"She is very kind." She wondered why he was asking all these questions.

"She has done marvels with you. That dress. Everything about you. Is she teaching you many things?"

"She's teaching me to sew."

"I wasn't thinking of sewing." He gave a little laugh.

"Oh?"

He reached over and pushed a stray lock of hair away from her face.

"Madame Collette is part French, you know. Wise in the ways of love," he said softly.

Desmond sat up straight, and lifted her chin.

"I don't know what you are talking about!"

He took hold of her shoulders, put his face very close to hers.

"Come, come, little girl, you've sailed with pirates. This dress, this coiffured hair can't disguise you, can't turn you overnight into a lady." His voice had lost it's softness.

Suddenly his hands slipped from her shoulders down to her tiny waist. He jerked her toward him and kissed her full on the lips.

She pulled her face away from his, reached up and slapped him.

"Let go of me! Let go of me this minute!" she said furiously.

"Why, you little tiger!" he grated.

She was wrestling now, as she had as a child with Forrester boys, and she had always been a good wrestler. And this young man did not try to force himself upon her as Alan had. He finally drew away from her and sat there rubbing his face where she had slapped him.

"I am not what you think I am!" Desmond cried. "I am not! I am not! No one can touch me, as you just did. No one. Except Dragon."

He gave her a long look, his sharp eyes full of surprise and almost amusement.

He said, "I am truly sorry, Desmond."

"Take me home, Mr. Kincaid."

25.

It took longer for the *Poinciana* to track down
the *Plume d'Or*, than it had the *Fleur de Lis*,
because the *Plume d'Or* had changed its
course. During the longer voyage Ian was able
to rest, to think, to wonder about his future.

The atmosphere of the ship gradually
changed. It became more of a warship than a
pirate ship. There was less roistering, less con-
sumption of rum. For the time being, at least,
the crew had become seamen, preparing to
fight for the crown instead of for themselves.
When Ian first told them they were about to attack another warship there had been grum-
bling. He promised them all rich rewards with
no idea of how he would produce such rewards. Perhaps the governor? He had hopes.

He wondered about his future, but he tried
not to dwell upon it. One thing at a time. One
more ship to capture.

Before, when he had gone to sea, it had been
something of an escape, an adventure: time on
the water which he loved, time to talk man
talk, to say what he thought, to lose his temper
if he felt like it, always with the knowledge

that Cabra was right there waiting for him—his wife, his home, the respect of the community. But now he wondered what Cabra would be like when he returned. What would he be like?

The capture of the *Plume d'Or* was much the same as the capture of the *Fleur de Lis* except that it was swifter—because of more men and more armament aboard the *Poinciana*. And this time there was no brave young defiant captain, but a philosophical older man who gave up his ship with a French shrug and allowed part of the *Poinciana* crew to sail it to Cabra.

Ian returned to Edwardsville with less of a feeling of triumph than before. He felt as if he had merely done a job.

There was no big welcoming committee at the dock this time. He could see only two lone figures as the *Poinciana* slipped into the harbor.

As the ship closed in on the dock, he recognized Jonathan and a woman.

At first he did not recognize her. She was wearing a long white dress that accentuated her golden tan. The yellow hair had been carefully pinned in place and topped by a white bonnet with a yellow feather dancing above it. Every inch the lady, except for those mischievous black eyes. He recognized the gold necklace she was wearing—her share of the booty on that long ago night.

He caught his breath. He had wondered about Desmond, wondered if she were happy living with Obediah. Or if some ardent young man had discovered her and swept her off her feet. On moonlit nights aboard ship he had thought of those bright eyes, that determined chin, the fire in that slender body. And here she was, metamorphosed. And with Jonathan!

He climbed down from the ship and walked over to them.

Desmond said, "Good afternoon, Dragon. Or are you Ian now?"

He managed to say. "Ian. Only Ian from now on."

Jonathan said, "Then the masquerade is over."

Ian looked at Jonathan. "Yes. the masquerade is over," he repeated.

"What next?" Jonathan asked.

"Frankly, I don't know. I am no longer a reverend. I am no longer a pirate." He looked at Desmond. "I am only a man."

"You are a hero, "Jonathan told him. "The governor wants to see you, at once."

As they walked up the street and along the waterfront Ian could feel the curiosity in the staring faces. They nodded greetings, a few even smiled, but he knew he had been the talk of Cabra for days. He remembered that Sunday when he had said, "There is drama in real life, too," and Jonathan had added, "Even here on Cabra."

Desmond was on the other side of Jonathan

as they proceeded to government house. Jonathan had taken her arm.

Ian said, "You two have become friends."

"Not as good friends as I should like." Jonathan's laugh was wry.

"Are you still with Obediah?" Ian asked her.

She shook her head. "He took me to live with Madame Collette."

She sounded shy. And she never had been shy with him before.

Governor Appleby was waiting for them in his office. When they walked in the governor stood up and put out his hand to Ian.

"Again, congratulations."

They shook hands.

Ian said, "The *Plume d'Or* is in the harbor. Its captain is a prisoner aboard the *Poinciana*."

"Good." The governor was obviously pleased.

"And now," Ian said, "I have a request."

Appleby's eyebrows went up. "Another horse? Another duel?" He smiled.

Ian shook his head. "It's the men. My crew. After all, most of them are buccaneers and they expect rewards. They've put up a good, hard fight."

"I see. And you?"

"No. I sailed as an Englishman, defending my homeland. Not as a privateer. Not this time."

He laid the papers he had taken from the *Plume d'Or* on the desk.

The governor said, "Your men will be rewarded. As Englishmen. Not as buccaneers."

"Thank you, your excellency." He turned to go.

"Rev ... Mr. Everett ..."

Ian turned around.

"You are an amazing man," the governor said. "You have continued to amaze me ever since I first knew that you were in charge when the *Fleur de Lis* was captured."

"How did you know?"

A rare smile jagged onto Appleby's goatlike face. "Kincaid here, told me."

"I see."

"I repeat, you are an amazing man, a heroic man. And heroes are rewarded. I'm giving you a grant of government land."

Desmond stepped forward and threw her arms around the governor's neck and kissed his cheek. He drew back in surprise.

The look of the lady had slipped from her as she, too, drew back in quick embarrassment and raised her face to Ian, almost the way she had looked at him the first time they met. And then the shyness faded and her expression was the same as the last time he saw her, when they said goodby on the hillside by the distillery, all love and longing.

He would not touch her now, he would say nothing, but he smiled down at her in a way he knew she would understand. Another place, another time, he had told her. Tomorrow. The whole future lay ahead of them. There was time. Time for everything.

With his eyes still on Desmond's face, he said, "Thank you, Governor Appleby. Thank you from the bottom of my heart. For the privilege of starting a new life."